MURDER

IN THE GARDEN DISTRICT

ALSO BY
GREG HERREN

THE CHANSE MACLEOD SERIES

Murder in the Rue Dauphine
Murder in the Rue St. Ann
Murder in the Rue Chartres
Murder in the Rue Ursulines

THE SCOTTY BRADLEY SERIES

Bourbon Street Blues
Jackson Square Jazz
Mardi Gras Mambo

MURDER
IN THE GARDEN DISTRICT

A CHANSE MACLEOD MYSTERY

GREG HERREN

ALYSON books

Murder in the Garden District
A Chanse MacLeod Mystery

Published by Alyson Books
245 West 17th Street, Suite 1200, New York, NY 10011
www.alyson.com

ALYSONbooks

First Alyson Books edition: October 2009

Library of Congress Cataloging-in-Publication data are on file.

ISBN-10: 1-59350-105-6
ISBN-13: 978-1-59350-105-1

10 9 8 7 6 5 4 3 2 1

Cover design by Victor Mingovits
Book interior by Jane Raese

Printed in the United States of America
Distributed by Consortium Book Sales and Distribution
Distribution in the United Kingdom by Turnaround Publisher
Services Ltd

This is for Stephen Driscoll

ACKNOWLEDGMENTS

As always, there are a lot of people to thank for their kindness, friendship, and support throughout the writing of this book.

First, I would like to thank Patrick Merla for assuming the unenviable task of not only being my editor but also having to do so in midstream. He was an absolute delight to work with and thoroughly professional.

Don Weise at Alyson is worthy of mention for tolerating my bizarre sense of humor and always answering my inane emails.

Julie Smith again provided her unique and delightful brand of cheerleading, coaching, cajoling, and threatening (but always with a smile) that helped keep me focused and moving on this book. Every writer should be so lucky as to have an Aunt Julie looking out for them—without her I'd still be a personal trainer with big dreams.

Jean Redmann has also been a source of inspiration and strength in my life now for (gulp) ten years. Thanks for everything, Jean—I still miss the Honda.

My co-workers at the NO/AIDS Task Force are an amazing group of people. Just being around them always improves my mood. Josh Fegley, Mark Drake (the Evil Mark), D. J. Jackson, Tanner Menard, Daniella Rivera, Martin Strickland, Eric Knudsen, and the always awesome Ked Dixon (Kedley) make me actually look forward to going to work every day. Diane Murray, Tia Tucker, and Maeghan Davis have enriched my life just by being in it. Thank you all so much.

My friends in Houston (Tom Wocken, Becky Cochrane, Timothy J. Lambert, Rhonda Rubin, Lindsay Smolensky, everyone at Murder by the Book, Margo, Guinness, Rexford, and Sugar) make every trip for a book signing over there something to look forward to rather than dread.

My friends in Fort Lauderdale (Stephen Driscoll, Stuart Wamsley, and Peggy Gentile) make every visit over there a joy.

A big thank you to my friends in Hammond (Michael Ledet, Patricia Brady, Bev and Butch Marshall) for their love, laughter, and generosity of spirit.

I also want to thank Lawrence Schimel, Laura Lippman, Nevada Barr, Philip Rafshoon, Poppy Z. Brite, Chris Debarr, John Angelico, Michael Carruth, Al and Harriet Campbell-Young, Mark Richards, Gillian Roger, Lee Pryor, Kenneth Holditch, Patty Friedman, Chris Wiltz, the Fabulous Carol Rosenfeld, everyone at Garden District Books (the Fabulous Deb, Awesome Amy, Ted Terrific, and Bossman Britton), Amie M. Evans, Thomas Keith, Ryan McNeeley, Jacob Rickoll, Gary Keener, Kathleen Bradean, David Pueterbaugh,

Mark G. Harris, Nathan Smith, Kelly Smith, Marianne Martin, Val McDermid, William J. Mann, Tim Miller, Alistair McCartney, Nancy Garden, Ellen Hart, Martin Hyatt, David Rosen, Robb Pearlman, Greg Wharton, Ian Philips, Steve Berman, and so many, many others for their support and thoughtfulness.

Marika Christian has been a great friend for almost twenty years.

And of course, Paul Willis makes my life worth living.

"It shows that we are not a package of rose leaves, that every interior inch of us is taken up with something ugly and functional and no room seems to be left for anything in there."

From *Summer and Smoke* by Tennessee Williams

" . . . Louisiana is not really an American state but a 'banana republic,' a Latin enclave of immorality set down in a country of Anglo-Saxon righteousness."

From *Huey Long* by T. Harry Williams

MURDER
IN
THE GARDEN DISTRICT

CHAPTER ONE

I CLIMBED OUT OF my car and immediately started sweating. *Christ*, I thought, tempted to loosen the uncharacteristic tie I was wearing, *this better be worth it*. I slammed the car door and headed for the front gate of the Palmer House. I'd been driving back from Houston when Barbara called, asking that I come by at four to meet a prospective client. She'd ordered me to wear a tie, which meant it was one of her society friends. And society friend meant deep pockets, which is always a good thing. I wiped the sweat off my forehead. *So much for making a good impression*, I thought as I opened the gate and headed up the walk to the house.

The Palmer House was a historic landmark of the Garden District, and also happened to be the home of my landlady and employer, Barbara Castlemaine, who'd inherited it from her first husband. Built before the Civil War, it was a monstrous-looking Italianate house painted a dark burgundy with black shutters. Black wrought iron lacework adorned the upper and lower galleries that ran around the house. The big brick fence that provided it with a semblance of privacy on two sides of the lot leaned toward the sidewalk at a gravity-defying angle from the immaculately kept lawn. A black wrought iron fountain bubbled in the center of a two-foot-high box hedge.

I rang the bell at precisely four o'clock. "Hey, Cora," I said when the door opened.

Cora had been Barbara's housekeeper for as long as I'd known her, and Barbara once told me that Cora had worked at the Palmer House since she was a teenager. I had no idea how old Cora was—her face was free of wrinkles and there were no signs of gray in her hair. She was wearing her black uniform with the white apron and little hat to match. Her face creased into a smile.

"Chanse! Always nice to see you." She lowered her voice and stepped onto the porch, pulling the door almost closed behind her. "How's your mama?"

I opened my mouth to give her my standard answer, and then closed it again. Her concern was written all over her face.

"Not good, Cora. She's responding to the treatments, but . . ." My voice trailed off. I forced a smile. "We'll see."

She took my hand and squeezed it. "I'm praying for you both."

I blinked away the excess water in my eyes. "Thank you."

"Come on, they're waiting for you in the drawing room."

I followed her into the house. All the sweat dried almost immediately in the frigid temperature inside the house. I shivered, wishing I'd brought a sweater with me. Cora led me down the hall past the hanging staircase and into the drawing room, where she announced me. Barbara was seated in a wingback chair facing the door. There was another woman in the room, sitting rigidly on a sofa with her back to me.

"Chanse, dear!"

Barbara called everyone *dear.* She rose and gave me a kiss on both cheeks. Now in her late fifties, she was still a beautiful woman. She refused to have any work done on her face, saying with a laugh, "I earned these lines!" Her thick blonde hair had strands of silver woven through it. She exercised every day to keep her figure. Even in jeans and a T-shirt, she managed to convey dignity and class. Today she was dressed in a simple black silk dress with a gold belt at the waist. She was wearing what she once jokingly referred to as her "power diamonds"—huge stones at her earlobes and a long chain around her neck ending in a large yellow teardrop diamond hanging between her breasts. But her face looked wan, as though she were under some kind of a strain, and I could see a nervous tic in her right cheek. She was using the phony tone of voice she usually reserved for people she didn't care for much.

"Allow me to introduce you to Cordelia Spencer Sheehan."

With a warning eye roll, she led me to the front of the couch.

What in the hell could this be about? I wondered.

I knew who she was, of course—who in New Orleans didn't? All you had to do was read the newspaper or watch the news occasionally. Louisiana's local version of royalty pursed her lips and extended a limp, white-gloved hand to me. I wasn't sure if she expected me to kiss it or shake it, so I took it and gave it an equally limp shake before dropping it.

Cordelia Spencer Sheehan appeared to be in her seventies. She had the extreme posture of royalty—her back ramrod straight and her shoulders held high and back. Her neck was fully extended, and even though she was seated, she gave the impression of looking down her nose at me. She wasn't classically beautiful. The nose was too prominent and her lips too thin. She was what most people would describe as striking. There were lines on her face, but the skin was still firm. She was slender and appeared to be short, but her presence made her seem much larger. Her white hair was immaculately styled and she wore a white silk blouse beneath a dove gray jacket. A rope of almost too large to be real pearls hung around her neck. Her skirt matched the jacket, and her legs were tastefully crossed at the ankles. Her blue eyes were sharp and alert as she took me in and apparently found me wanting.

"It's nice to meet you, Mrs. Sheehan," I said, a little intimidated.

"Mr. MacLeod." She inclined her head slightly downward in a disdainful nod, and turned her eyes to Barbara. "You may leave us now, Barbara."

Her tone was dismissive, like Barbara was a servant.

Barbara didn't react the way I expected her to. She inclined her head respectfully and said, "Of course." As she pulled the door closed behind her, she gave me an apologetic look and shrugged her shoulders.

I sat down in the wingback chair Barbara had vacated.

"Barbara tells me you need my help."

"With no offense or disrespect intended, Mr. MacLeod, I cannot express how distasteful this entire matter is to me. I never thought I would see the day when I would require the services of a private investigator. My son, Wendell, was murdered last night in our home. He was shot to death."

That got my attention.

"And I seem to have gotten myself into a bit of a mess which Barbara assures me you can assist me with."

Her face and voice were completely without emotion. Her eyes never left mine.

"I'm sorry for your loss, Mrs. Sheehan," I said carefully.

The Sheehans were to Louisiana what the Kennedys were to Massachusetts. They'd been actively involved in state and national politics since before the Civil War. The family had produced state and city legislators, mayors, governors, senators, and congressmen. The woman sitting across the coffee table from me was the daughter of a two-term governor and had also been married to a two-term governor, Bobby Sheehan. He'd died of cancer shortly after leaving office. After

his death, Cordelia Spencer Sheehan had devoted herself to helping domestic-abuse victims. Her foundation,
named for her late husband, operated several shelters
not just in New Orleans but throughout the state. She'd
been recognized for her contributions numerous times.
Just a few months ago, she'd gotten some honor from
the current governor that had been splashed all over
the *Times-Picayune.* Her son, Wendell Sheehan, had
been attorney general of Louisiana back in the '90s and
had served on the City Council and in the state Senate. He had run unsuccessfully for mayor in the election after the hurricane, and was rumored to be eying
the Senate seat currently held by a Republican from
Metairie with a penchant for prostitutes. His political
enemies often contemptuously called him a *liberal*, like
that should automatically disqualify him for office. I'd
voted for him for mayor, and would have gladly voted
for him again for the Senate.

I waited for her to go on. The silence became a bit
awkward, so I asked, "Who do the police—"

"That's part of the problem, you see." A small smile
cracked her façade, but disappeared so quickly I wasn't
sure I hadn't imagined it. "I am afraid they may think
I did it."

My heartbeat accelerated. "Perhaps you should start
at the beginning," I said, leaning back in my chair and
taking out a pen and the notepad I kept tucked into my
pants pocket.

She inhaled dramatically. "As you know, there was
a terrible thunderstorm last night. I was in my room at

home, reading. It was late, around eleven-thirty." She cleared her throat. "I have trouble falling asleep at night, so I often read. My son wasn't home—he's been coming home late a lot lately. He is—*was*—looking into the feasibility of running for the United States Senate, and had opened a campaign office. I was reading in my room when I heard the shot." She closed her eyes, and her left hand went to her throat. "You can only imagine how terrified I was. My first thought was of course for the children. I had no idea what had happened, if there was a burglar in the house or what. I put on my robe and went into the hallway. My granddaughter Alais—Wendell's daughter—was just coming out of her room. I told her to stay upstairs and call the police. The poor dear was terrified. I opened my grandson Carey's door to make sure he was okay, but he was wearing headphones and apparently hadn't heard anything. He didn't even notice me. So I shut the door and went downstairs."

"The shot came from downstairs?"

"Yes."

"Go on."

She gave me a withering look. "As I said, I went downstairs. The front door was wide open, and there was water all over the hallway floor—tracked in, possibly by my son. When I got to the bottom of the staircase . . ." She closed her eyes. "I could see my son lying in a pool of blood in the drawing room. I immediately rushed to his side, but there was no pulse. I saw the gun lying there, and I picked it up."

"You picked it up?" That hadn't been smart, and she

didn't strike me as being a stupid woman. But then, if I was to believe what she said, she'd gone downstairs without knowing if it was safe.

She met my gaze without blinking. "I wasn't thinking clearly. I must have been in shock. When I picked it up the gun went off again. The bullet went into the floor." Her hands balled into fists. "As I was standing there, my daughter-in-law walked into the room. I immediately knew what had happened." She pursed her lips again. It was clear she didn't care for her son's wife. "She said she'd called the police already."

"You didn't see or hear anyone else?"

She shook her head.

"And outside of the family, there was no one else in the house?"

"Not as far as I knew."

"And what do you think had happened?"

"His wife shot him, of course." Mrs. Sheehan didn't bother to try to mask her contempt as she spat the words at me. "And that's why I need you, Mr. MacLeod. I've already retained an attorney named Loren McKeithen, and he recommended you. He advised me to have Barbara work as a go-between."

I must have frowned.

"Apparently you aren't fond of Mr. McKeithen?" Her lips curled in what might have been considered a smile.

"We've had our differences," I said cautiously. "But I can work with Loren."

Loren was the one who'd gotten me into a mess

a year ago. He'd brought me into another case, and turned on me when he didn't like what I discovered. I didn't trust him.

"Good. The most important thing here is to protect my daughter-in-law, and the two of you will need to work together."

The words sounded hollow to me. And she wasn't making sense.

"But you picked up the gun," I said. "You should be more concerned about—"

Her eyes narrowed. "I wasn't thinking clearly," she snapped. "I didn't kill my son. The notion is ridiculous. Only a fool would think I killed my own child. Obviously it was his wife. After all, it was her gun. Who else could it have been?" Her lips tightened.

I pitied the district attorney who might have to cross-examine her.

"How do you know it was her gun?"

"She told the police it was hers."

"Did you wipe the gun when you picked it up?"

"Why would I do such a stupid thing?"

"I would think you'd be a little more concerned about having your fingerprints on the gun," I said, resisting the urge to point out that picking it up in the first place had been incredibly stupid.

"They did a test of some sort on my hands." She waved a hand. "To see if I'd fired the gun. Of course, I explained how that all happened." Her smile chilled me. "The idiots didn't test my daughter-in-law's hands, even though I told them she'd killed him."

"What does she say?"

"She told them I killed him," she sneered, "which is utter nonsense. *She's* the one with everything to gain."

"I'll need to speak with her."

"You have an appointment tomorrow morning at ten to discuss all of that—and her *ridiculous* story—at our home."

She handed me a gold-embossed card with her name and address on it, then waved her gloved hand dismissively.

"I will pay you, of course, quite handsomely, through Mr. McKeithen's office. Say, a thousand dollars a day plus expenses?"

That was almost three times my going rate. "That's very generous," I replied cautiously.

I've always been suspicious of overly generous clients. They tend to take it for granted that I'll be willing to break the law on their behalf. I may bend the law on occasion, but I won't do anything that might put me behind bars.

She went on as though I hadn't said a word, her gloved fingers tapping a steady tattoo on the couch arm.

"I'm paying you to devote yourself entirely to this case, Mr. MacLeod, to the exclusion of all else, so I cannot expect you to not be compensated properly. I know you work for Barbara's company, but she understands how important this is. And I expect results. There will also be a substantial bonus for those results."

"I don't understand," I said. "What kind of result

are you looking for? Proving your daughter-in-law is guilty?"

She started laughing. It was a very unpleasant sound. She put her hand to her throat.

"Oh, dear me. My daughter-in-law killed my son, Mr. MacLeod. There's no question about that." Her eyes flashed angrily. "*Your* job is to find reasonable doubt for the jury, enough maybe to keep the district attorney from prosecuting her. That's what I'm paying you for."

I looked her square in the eyes.

"You handled the murder weapon. You even fired it. Even if, as you say, *only a fool* would think you'd shot him, that's enough reasonable doubt right there to keep your daughter-in-law out of jail. Loren is a damned good lawyer—he'd have a field day with that."

"Let me make myself clear, Mr. MacLeod," she said contemptuously. "As long as there is breath in my body, no one named Sheehan will go to prison for anything. No matter what I might think of her and what she has done, my daughter-in-law is a member of my family, and I will do everything in my power to ensure that she does not spend a single night behind bars for her crime—no matter how much I would enjoy seeing that happen. And I am not about to be painted as a *murderer* in a court of law to save her. My son had plenty of enemies. I want you to look outside my family. Is that clear?"

She stood up and walked to the door. "Ten o'clock tomorrow morning, Mr. MacLeod," she said, turning back to me. "Do be punctual."

I heard her heels click softly in the hallway as the door closed behind her.

I poured myself a gin and tonic from the little bar in a corner of the room. It was at my lips when Barbara said from the doorway, "Pour me one of those, will you, dear? That woman would drive anyone to drink."

Barbara took the glass from me and plopped down on the sofa. I'd never seen her drink anything other than champagne—usually mixed with orange juice. She tossed the drink back like it was nothing and set the glass down on the coffee table.

"I'm sorry to get you involved with that awful woman, but I didn't have a choice," she said.

I sat in the wingback chair again. "What do you mean, you didn't have a choice?"

"Let's just say I owe her and leave it at that." Barbara closed her eyes. "I am truly sorry, Chanse, dear. I hope you don't come to regret working for her, like everyone else who deals with her. But please don't ask me to say any more."

I knew better than to press her.

As the owner of Crown Oil, Barbara was the wealthiest person in Louisiana. We'd been working together for years. She'd started out as my client, when she was being blackmailed and hired me to help her. She'd slept with a pair of underage bodybuilding twins and there were pictures. The whole thing had been a setup. I'd gotten the pictures and negatives back for her and she had put me on the payroll of Crown Oil as a consultant. I did quarterly checks of the security systems at their refineries and other facilities, and made recommendations for improvements. I did background checks of prospective executives and board members, drawing on my contacts and two years' experience working in the New Orleans police department. She'd also had me check out several men she became involved with later—when you're the richest woman in the state, you become a target for fortune hunters. In return for these services she paid me a generous salary, more than enough to support my own investigation business and pay an assistant, considering that she owned my building and only charged me $100 a month rent for an apartment worth $1,200. In addition to the cushy consulting job, she brought me clients. I wasn't about to upset the apple cart unnecessarily.

I decided to get whatever basic information I could about the Sheehans and continue making notes.

"They all lived in the same house?" I asked Barbara. "That must have been uncomfortable."

"It's Cordelia's house and she wouldn't hear of them living elsewhere. Everything is Cordelia's. She controls the money. Wendell had none of his own. I'm sure he hoped she'd die every day of his life. Imagine having *that* for your mother. I'd hang myself after twenty-four hours in that place."

"Did she tell you anything about what happened?"

"Just that Janna killed Wendell, and she needed a private eye whose discretion could be counted on. She knew about you—that damned Loren McKeithen sent her to me."

I felt sorry for Loren for a moment. Barbara would make him pay for this.

"I'd say Cordelia should be more worried about herself than about her daughter-in-law. She not only handled the gun, she fired it. At least, that's her story. I take it she didn't tell you that."

Barbara smiled. "Well, well, well. She left that out. Seems like Cordelia's gotten herself into a bit of trouble." She seemed to enjoy the idea.

I wondered what exactly she *owed* Cordelia for. It was obvious she detested the woman.

"But knowing Cordelia, I'm sure she thinks no one would ever think she'd commit murder," she added.

"You nailed that one right on the head," I said. "Do you know the widow?"

"Janna? Yes, I know Janna. The poor thing had no idea what she was marrying into. I felt sorry for her. I still do."

She got up and poured herself another gin and tonic. Mostly it was gin, with a bit of tonic splashed in the glass.

"She was what Cordelia and her sort consider a nobody—unsuitable to marry the heir to the throne. She was only in her mid-twenties when she married Wendell. She was one of his secretaries. You could have knocked us all down with a feather when it happened. I'd always assumed that if he married again it would be Monica Davis—and I'm sure Monica thought so too."

"And she is?"

"Monica teaches political science at Tulane. She'd been with Wendell for years—some say even before his first wife died. I heard that the two of them had started up again, but that could just be talk. You know how people are—and no one really liked Janna very much, the poor thing."

"Why not?"

Barbara fixed her green eyes on me. "She was from Hammond, Chanse. She had no pedigree. Her father was a janitor. She was never a debutante, never a maid or Queen of Comus or Momus or Rex. Everyone looked down on her—the same way they did me when I married Roger Palmer. I tried to be nice to her, take her under my wing, but she wouldn't have anything to do with me. I'm sure Cordelia told her a lot of unpleasant things about me. But I could understand what she was going through, because I'd been through it myself. Until, of course, I married Charles Castlemaine and suddenly had more money than God at my disposal. The power of being richer than they are can never be underestimated." She gave me a hard smile. "They're polite to me now, but I'm not one of them. I never will be. And neither will Janna."

"Do you think she could have killed him?"

Barbara didn't answer me at first, and when she finally spoke, she didn't look at me.

"He was a horrible man, Chanse, an absolutely horrible man. Every bit as awful as his mother. If Janna did kill him—and I am not saying she did—I'm certain she had her reasons."

She glanced at her watch.

"Good Lord, I have to get running. I have a meeting in half an hour."

She rose and walked quickly to the door.

"You can see yourself out, can't you, dear? And again, I am so sorry." She winked at me. "I promise to make it up to you."

As I sat in my car waiting for the air-conditioning to kick into gear, I called my research assistant, Abby Grosjean. "We got a job," I said when she answered. "I need you to find everything you can on Wendell Sheehan, his wife, Janna—hell, anything you can find out about the entire Sheehan family."

"Wendell Sheehan was killed last night," Abby said. "It's all over the news."

"That's right," I said. "We're working for the Sheehan family." I looked at Barbara's house. "I need it as soon as possible. And while you're at it, find out everything you can about Barbara Castlemaine."

"The *boss*? Are you sure?"

"I'm sure."

I'd never checked out Barbara before. I'd always considered it an invasion of her privacy. I knew some of her secrets, of course—you couldn't work as a private eye for someone as long as I'd worked for Barbara without learning some things about her. And from time to time she'd let something personal slip. But I'd never done a background check on her, and now my curiosity was piqued. She obviously hated Cordelia Spencer Sheehan and her son. So why would she do her a favor?

Maybe I should just leave Barbara alone—she might not appreciate the intrusion into her privacy, and she was certainly my golden goose. I'd be up shit creek if I lost the Crown Oil gig, and with Abby on salary now, it wasn't just me that would be affected.

Then again, Cordelia had something on her—and for Barbara to put up with the dismissive way the old woman treated her, it had to be something really bad. Truth be told, if I was careful, the only way Barbara would find out was if I told her—and I could make that decision later.

As for Janna Sheehan, it would be interesting to meet her. I already felt a little sorry for her—under the best of circumstances it couldn't be easy to be that woman's daughter-in-law.

I parked in the lot alongside my house and went into the living room of my apartment on the first floor in the front of the building. Plopping down on the sofa, I called my best friend, Paige.

Paige and I went back all the way to our college days at LSU, which now seemed a million years ago. She'd been a reporter for the *Times-Picayune* until last year, when she'd accepted the job as editor-in-chief at *Crescent City*. In that short time she'd turned the glossy monthly from a barely break-even piece of fluff into a must-read for locals. When she'd been at the *Times-Picayune*, she'd often pulled information from the morgue for me, and while she didn't have that same kind of access at *Crescent City*, she might know someone at the paper who would do her a favor. She answered on the first ring, breathless.

"Chanse! I can't talk long—deadline looming. How's your mother? How are you?"

"Hanging in there, and my mother . . ."

I hesitated. Paige had been the one to convince me to go to see her in the first place.

"She's responding to the treatments, but who knows?"

"I'm so sorry . . . Look, Chanse, it's really crazy around here right now. Why don't I stop by later with dinner? Ryan's visiting the kids tonight."

Ryan Tujague was her boyfriend. His ex-wife and two kids had lived in Mandeville since Katrina.

"Have you heard about Wendell Sheehan?" she continued, seemingly changing the subject. "He would have to go and get himself killed right before we put the magazine to bed. Everyone around here is wondering if we'll have jobs tomorrow."

"What does Wendell Sheehan's murder have to do with the magazine?" I asked.

"Do you ever listen when I talk to you, Chanse? The Sheehans own the Crescent City Publishing Group. I mean, he stepped down as publisher in order to launch his Senate campaign, shortly after I came to work here, but he was the one who hired me. Who knows what's going to happen now, or who's going to be in charge? I just pray to God it's not his mother. But she never shows her face here. Rachel's fit to be tied."

Rachel Delesdernier was *Crescent City*'s new publisher. I'd never met her, but Paige loved working for her. I decided not to tell her she'd never mentioned

Wendell Sheehan to me before, or that Cordelia Spencer Sheehan had hired me, at least not yet.

"I'll tell you about my mom over dinner," I said. "It seems like forever since I've seen you."

The job did take a toll on her private life. Paige often worked twelve to sixteen hours a day without time off for weeks on end. It was causing problems with Ryan, as well.

"Plan on me being there around seven. If we don't have the magazine done by then, heads will roll."

She hung up.

I grabbed an empty manila folder from the box on the bookcase next to my desk and wrote SHEEHAN on the flap, then opened a new document on my computer. I typed in the pertinent information—date and time hired, rate of pay, client, task—and stared at the cursor for a moment, hearing Mrs. Sheehan in my head.

I want you to look outside my family. My son had a lot of enemies. Of course she did it! But as long as there is breath in my body, no member of this family is going to spend a single night in jail.

Maybe it was my years in the NOPD, but I didn't like the idea of helping someone get away with murder. It was why I had never considered going to law school. I have very clear opinions about people who commit crimes. You do the crime, you do the time. The notion that there was a separate justice for the rich went against everything I believed in.

But something else was bothering me. Cordelia

Spencer Sheehan might be any number of things, but she was not stupid. So why, if she was innocent, would she pick up the gun that had obviously been used to kill her son? Even if she was in shock, as she claimed, it wasn't natural. The *natural* thing would have been to scream, or go to her child, or even faint. Why on earth did she pick up the gun?

Maybe she honestly believed that despite the evidence, her word would be enough for the police and the district attorney. And maybe she was right. She was rich, powerful, and well respected throughout the state. She was also well connected. Probably she could use her pull to quash the investigation. That was how things worked in Louisiana.

So why hire me?

There was a hell of a lot more here than I was being told. I also wasn't convinced that what she'd said was true. My instinct was to remove myself from the case. I don't like it when clients lie to me, especially when the lies are so obvious they wouldn't fool anyone. They certainly wouldn't fool the police.

"Stick to the facts, Chanse," I said out loud. "It's entirely possible she did exactly what she said she did. Smart people have done stupider things."

And then there was the Barbara angle. For whatever reason, she *owed* Cordelia, and was using me to pay off that debt. I certainly owed Barbara a lot myself. The least I could do was get that awful woman off her back.

But Cordelia Spencer Sheehan didn't strike me as the sort who would forget whatever debt Barbara owed her just because I'd taken on this case. Whatever she had on Barbara gave her power over her, and Cordelia Spencer Sheehan enjoyed power and control. She kept her entire family on a leash. Life in that house must be one hell of a freak show.

It was time to get to work.

CHAPTER TWO

JANNA SHEEHAN WAS A beautiful woman, despite the dark circles under her gray eyes. In her early thirties, with long, thick auburn hair, she had clear, smooth skin the color of white porcelain. I could see blue veins in her long throat. She was short, barely five feet tall, with a tiny waist and ample hips. She looked as though she weighed less than a hundred pounds. Given the size of her frame, her breasts seemed almost too large to be real underneath her green Tulane T-shirt.

We were sitting in a gazebo behind the Sheehan mansion on St. Charles Avenue. A ceiling fan whirred overhead, but it wasn't providing enough breeze to keep me from sweating, and the glass of iced tea wasn't helping any more than the fan. My shirt was soaked. Janna had led me out here so we could speak without being overheard by anyone. I'd thought it odd, but acquiesced.

She blew a cloud of smoke out of her mouth and gave me a brittle smile. "Of course she killed him," she said. "But how would I know why? Cordelia doesn't share that kind of information with me."

"Just tell me what happened the night of the murder."

She flicked ash into a green glass ashtray. "I was waiting up for Wendell. He'd been coming home late more and more, saying he was working on strategy and so forth for the campaign. Whether he was doing that or not, I don't know. I had my suspicions. He often came home smelling like a brewery." She gave me a tired look. "I didn't much care one way or the other, but that night I needed to talk to him. I'd been putting it off for a while and it was getting to the point I couldn't wait any longer. I was in my room—it's right at the top of the stairs, the first door—and I saw his headlights from my window. I went to the window and saw him get out of the car in the rain. He was drunk again. I got scared and decided it could wait another night."

"You were afraid of your husband?"

"Does that surprise you? It's why I bought the gun in the first place."

"Had he been violent with you?"

She looked down and nodded. "Only when he was drinking," she said quietly. "Anyway, it wasn't too long after that I heard the first shot."

"What did you do then?"

She raised her head and looked me in the eyes. "I was terrified. I called 911, then opened my door and looked out—to try to see what was going on. Alais and Carey's doors were closed, and I could see the front door was open. The house was silent. I don't think I've ever been so scared in my life. But I couldn't just stay there. I was about halfway down the stairs when I heard the second shot. I ran the rest of the way, and saw Cordelia in the drawing room with a gun in her hands. And then I saw Wendell. I think I may have screamed." Her body shook for a moment. "And then the police came," she whispered.

"Did you know it was your gun?"

She smiled weakly. "The police told me later. My initials are engraved in the handle." She shook her head bitterly. "Obviously, Cordelia took it to frame me. Why else would she use my gun? There are enough guns in the house to hold off the Yankee army. She probably never thought I'd get downstairs fast enough to catch her in the act. The gun would have my fingerprints on it, wouldn't it? My guess is that she was going to shoot him, drop the gun, and then pretend to find the body. Unfortunately, I got downstairs before she could finish setting me up."

She refilled her glass from the sweating pitcher of iced tea on the table between us.

Cordelia had said that Janna told the police it was her gun. I decided to play along and see what else she had to say.

"Mrs. Sheehan—"

"Janna," she interrupted me. "Cordelia is Mrs. Sheehan. I'm just plain Janna."

"All right, Janna." I gave her what I hoped was a reassuring smile. "It wasn't very smart to go downstairs. You should have stayed in your room until the police came."

"Good thing I didn't. If I hadn't caught her in the act, I'd be in a cell right now."

"You didn't think to at least take a weapon with you? If there are so many guns in the house—"

She took another drink. "I looked for my gun but it wasn't there. So I took the fireplace poker from my room."

That made even less sense. I changed tack.

"You and your mother-in-law didn't get along?"

She barked out a harsh laugh. "Cordelia was *delighted* when her son married a nobody. She welcomed me into the family with open arms." She viciously crushed her cigarette in the ashtray. "But seriously, it was a year before she finally stopped referring to me as 'Wendell's mistake.' She had big plans for the Crown Prince. This Senate race was just the start. She thought that I'd embarrass him somehow. Like I was too stupid to be nice to everyone and keep my mouth shut about policy. Please. It wasn't my fault he lost the mayoral race, no matter how much she blamed me for it. My role was to look pretty and smile a lot, play the adoring wife. And I did it well."

"Your husband stepped out of public life after serving one term as attorney general, and didn't return until the 2006 mayoral race. Why was there such a long break in his political career?"

"Grace died. His first wife. Alais's mother."

She took another cigarette from the pack, looked at it, and returned it to the pack.

"He never talked about it, I never asked. All I know is

she died, and he left politics for a while. Around here, sometimes it's better not to know things."

That was interesting. "How long after she died before he married you?"

"Four or five years, I think."

She looked past me and stood up. I turned in my chair and saw a teenager walking across the lawn toward us, his head down, as though he was fascinated with the white Air Jordans on his feet. He appeared to be about thirteen or so, tall and gangly, his arms and legs barely skin and bone, ending in enormous feet and hands, in an oversized Coldplay T-shirt and a pair of long checkered shorts that almost reached his knobby knees. His hair was so blond it looked white, and he had the same pale skin as Janna. I suppressed a grin. I'd been tall and skinny when I was that age. As he climbed the steps into the gazebo, I noticed the white down on his bare legs and a rash of pimples across his cheek. He stared at Janna, his lower lip sticking out in an angry pout, towering over her as I had over my own mother at that age. Like Janna, he had dark circles under his blue eyes.

"It's time for swim practice, Mom," he mumbled, barely audible. "Grandma says it's not a good idea."

He didn't acknowledge my presence with so much as a glance.

"All right, Carey." She nodded to me. "Carey, this is Chanse MacLeod, the investigator your grandmother hired."

"How do you do." He still didn't look at me. "Can I go to practice, Mom?" he mumbled, a plea in his voice.

Her jaw tightened; her lips compressed into a tight line that she forced into a big smile that didn't reach her eyes.

"Fortunately, she's not your mother. It's fine with me. It'll do you some good to get out of the house. Go."

His face lit up. "Thanks, Mom!" He bent down and kissed her cheek, and was gone in a rushed tangle of arms and legs.

She watched him go. The smile on her face didn't fade until I heard the door to the main house slam behind me. She turned back to me, her eyes flashing angrily.

"Cordelia thinks we should lock ourselves up to mourn properly. Carey's thirteen and I'd rather he spend a few hours in the pool with his mind on something else than mope around this house." She gave me a rather ugly smile. "He's *my* son, no matter how much she wants to forget that."

"Are they close?"

Her voice softened. "I'll give her that, she treats Carey like he's blood. She always has. It's his mother she has a problem with."

"How long were you and Wendell married?"

This time she lit the cigarette. "Wendell wasn't Carey's father, if that's where you're going with this. Wendell adopted him after we were married."

"And Carey's father?"

"Carey's father has nothing to do with this. That's ancient history, and there's no need to dredge it all up again." She blew smoke at me. "I was nineteen, and we weren't married. We'll just leave it at that."

I was curious why Janna didn't want to talk about his biological father, but changed the subject. I could have Abby get a copy of Carey's birth certificate.

"So, what was so important that night that you had to talk to Wendell about?"

"My marriage was a mess," she said harshly. "If there was any way I could have, I would have left him and gotten a divorce. The marriage had been over for several years. But Wendell—and his mother—worried about what it might do to his campaign. A divorce might hurt his attacks on the Metairie whoremonger if he didn't have a loving wife at his side. And the campaign was the important thing, you know."

"You didn't need their permission to get a divorce," I pointed out.

Her eyes flashed. "That's true. I signed a prenup—Cordelia saw to *that*—so I would get nothing in a divorce." She seemed to deflate. "How could I fight them for my kids with no money? A few months ago, I packed some suitcases and checked into the Monteleone, to figure things out. *She* came to see me and ordered me to come back. She told me if I tried to get a divorce, if I ruined his chances at this Senate seat, they'd fight for full custody of the children. I couldn't abandon the kids like that, Mr. MacLeod. No matter how bad it was for me here, I had no chance in court against them. They have the money, the power, and the connections. I'd never see my kids again. And I would *never* leave those kids in their hands. Look at the great job Cordelia did with Wendell. She wasn't going to be in charge of *my* kids. So I came back."

"You're close to your stepdaughter?"

"I couldn't love Alais more if she were mine."

She pulled another cigarette from the pack and lit it.

"If Wendell had his way, Alais would be up at Ole Miss right now. *I* stood up to him, convinced him she needed a semester off. He didn't care about her, he never did. And Cordelia? Alais is a girl, useless to her and her plans. Cordelia is hopelessly old-fashioned. Even with Mary Landrieu in the Senate, it never occurred to her that Alais could go into politics. Not that she wanted to.

"I was stupid to think they'd let me go. And I know my saying that gives me a motive—I couldn't get a divorce so I had to kill him, right? But I didn't kill him. Cordelia did. And no matter how hard she tries to pin this on me, she can't. Because the truth is she killed him. I saw her with the gun." A weak smile played at her lips. "And won't the truth set me free?"

I debated with myself about telling her that Cordelia had hired me to throw suspicion elsewhere. Surely Janna must know this. But then why act as though she didn't? I decided to keep playing along.

"When did you and Wendell start having problems?"

Janna unfolded her arms and looked over my shoulder. "When I married him, it was like an old movie, you know? The secretary marries the boss and lives happily ever after. But those movies never show what it's like *after* the wedding. There's a reason why that doesn't happen very often in real life. Men from the Garden District shouldn't marry janitors' daughters from Hammond. True love doesn't conquer all. That's for fairy tales, lies they tell little girls. I didn't fit in. I didn't belong here. But when Wendell loved me I could deal with the snide looks and snubs and whispers. I could even handle Cordelia."

She drummed her fingernails on the table. "Cordelia hated me from the moment I arrived in her precious house on the Avenue, the miserable old bitch, no matter how much I tried to fit in. It took about four years for me to realize that Wendell married me precisely because I *didn't*, to rebel against his mother. The more I changed—the more I learned about spoons and forks and how a Garden District wife is supposed to act and behave—the less he liked it. Do you know what he told me once? *If I'd wanted my wife to be a lady, I would have married the real thing.*"

The pain in her eyes was difficult to bear, so I looked down at my hands. "And it eventually became physical?" I asked softly.

"About three years ago, when our marriage began to fail, he became abusive. At first it was emotional—insulting me in front of people, demeaning me in any way he could think of—and then it became physical. Four months ago, he came home drunk one night, and we argued. He called me every name in the book. And then—" She grabbed the edge of the table. "He raped me."

She held up her right hand. It was shaking. A tear rolled out of her left eye and slid down her face. She took a deep breath, wiped her face, and went on.

"He also sprained my wrist. That's when I left. After Cordelia forced me to come back, I bought a gun and began taking lessons at the firing range in Metairie. That wasn't going to happen again. Ever."

"I'm sorry," I said lamely. "We can finish this another time."

She had the grace to give me a weak smile. "Thank you," she said, touching my hand. "But no. It helps to talk about it."

I reached for her hand, but decided it might not be appropriate to take it. "Then please take me through it, every detail. You said you were waiting up for him that night. You had something you wanted to talk to him about?"

"I had some news for him I'd been putting off for several days, but I knew I couldn't keep it from him forever. Especially not in *this* house. I'd decided to wait up for him, no matter how late he was, and talk to him. In spite of everything, I still loved him. I know that sounds crazy."

She shook her head, and looked down at her hands. She was tearing a paper coaster to shreds. She took a drink from her water glass.

"I thought my news would change things. If I couldn't get a divorce, if we had to stay married, I thought surely we could work something out. It would never be what it was before, but we had to be able to come to some kind of understanding."

"And what was your news?"

She went on like I'd not said a word. "It was about eleven-thirty, I think, when his car pulled into the driveway. My bedroom windows open on the driveway, so I saw his headlights. I went to the window and looked out. I watched him get out of his car in the rain, and I could tell he was drunk again. Such an idiot. We couldn't get a divorce because of how it might look, but he didn't have a problem risking a ticket every night for driving drunk. If he and Cordelia could just get their minds out of the 1950s they'd have realized that divorce is not a death sentence in politics. Ronald Reagan was divorced, for God's sake. But a drunk driving arrest? Kiss your political ass goodbye. I might be a nobody from the North Shore, as Cordelia likes to remind me at every opportunity, but I do know that much."

"So, he was drunk?" I made a note to get a copy of the autopsy report.

"Oh, yes. I went to my desk to get my gun, but it wasn't in the drawer."

"So, you knew the gun was gone before you heard the shots?"

She looked down at her hands. The silence became uncomfortable.

"Yes." Her voice was practically a whisper.

My lips pressed together. Cordelia Spencer Sheehan had just gotten an award from the governor for her work with abused women—and her daughter-in-law was being abused right under her nose.

"Did Cordelia know about the abuse?"

"She isn't deaf, dumb, and blind." Janna's voice was brittle. "If it weren't for the kids, I would have gone to one of those shelters she raises all that money for. Maybe I should have. Talk about scandal! But she always reminded me that his career was more important. *Think of all the good he's going to do when he's in the Senate.*" She mimicked Cordelia's voice perfectly. "He was still a monster."

"And when you saw that your gun wasn't there?"

"I decided that the talk with Wendell could wait. I didn't know how he'd react, but I wasn't going to let myself be hurt again."

She sounded resigned, defeated. She took another drink of tea.

"At that time, did you wonder what had happened to the gun?"

"I didn't think about it. All that mattered was that it wasn't there. I figured Wendell had taken it. That was his style."

She looked out over the lawn again.

"Go on," I said gently.

"I turned off my lights and locked my bedroom door and went to bed. Until I heard the gunshot."

"And then what happened?"

"It startled me. I'd fired the gun enough times to know what it sounded like." She balled her hands into fists. "I got out of bed, unlocked my door, and called 911. I was on the stairs when I heard the second shot. I went to the drawing room and saw Wendell lying on the floor with blood everywhere. Cordelia was standing, with the gun in her hands, looking at him. And then she saw me. She dropped the gun and said something about calling the police. I told her I already had, that they were on their way."

She closed her eyes and shuddered.

"I checked for a pulse, and there wasn't one. I went across the hall to the library to wait for the police to show up. That was when I noticed that the front door was open, and there was water all over the floor. I assumed Wendell had tracked it in—it was really pouring outside. But I couldn't understand why he didn't close the door behind him. Too drunk, I suppose."

"Who else was in the house?"

"Cordelia, of course, and the kids. They'd gone up to their rooms after dinner. About ten, I went in to say good night to them in their rooms." She smiled faintly. "Carey had his headphones on, he always does. Alais was already asleep."

"Anyone else?"

"We don't have live-in help—Vernita, the one who let you in, leaves every day at six—and ever since Rachel and Quentin moved out—"

"Rachel and Quentin?"

"Quentin is Wendell's cousin, and Rachel is his wife. They moved out about a month ago. Wendell didn't much care for them, and even though they were in the pool house—"

She pointed behind me. The small building was just beyond the pool.

"It was still too close, as far as Wendell was concerned."

"And there was no one else in the house?" I pressed.

"Not to my knowledge."

"Do you know where the children were?"

"They said they were in their rooms."

"They didn't hear the shots?"

"I assume they had their headphones on. They always do."

"And they all had access to your gun?"

"I never lock my room unless I am going to bed," she said. "So, yes, they could have. Vernita and the maid who comes twice a week had access to it as well, obviously, whenever they were in the house."

"When was the last time you saw the gun?"

"I went to the shooting range three days ago. When I got back, I cleaned it and put it away."

"When you found your husband, did you see or hear or notice anything out of the ordinary?"

"Besides my husband's body? I wasn't really paying attention. I was in shock. The police found the safe in the drawing room was open—"

Cordelia hadn't mentioned anything about the safe. Given her instructions, I found this odd. If the safe was open, there was a possibility that Wendell had caught someone robbing it. But how would a burglar have gotten Janna's gun? A half-decent lawyer could convince a jury someone else could have killed Wendell, even with Cordelia picking up the gun.

"Was anything missing?" I asked. "Had the safe been broken into?"

"I wouldn't know. I didn't have access to the safe. Any jewelry I had that was worth anything is in a safety deposit box at the bank. Wendell never gave me the combination to the safe. I have no idea what he and Cordelia kept in there. You'd have to ask her. Or the police."

I moved on. "You said that it was about three years ago that your marriage troubles started. Around the time of Katrina?"

"That didn't help, but no, the trouble started before then, in the spring, right after Mardi Gras, I think." She closed her eyes, thinking back, and opened them again. "Yes, things started to deteriorate around then."

"Any idea why?"

She went to the sideboard and poured herself a glass of ice water, took a long drink, then sat down and faced me again.

"The initial problem was Carey, my son. You have to understand a few things about this family, all right? Cordelia's family, the Spencers—well, they were the closest thing to royalty we had in Louisiana, and she was the last one of them. When she was young, things were different. The notion of Cordelia carrying the family banner into politics was just not possible. So her father married her off to Willy Sheehan. The Sheehans were another political family, just not as prominent or as long established as the Spencers. All the Spencer eggs were put in the Sheehan basket, if you want to mix a metaphor. Wendell was their only son. His cousin Quentin had no interest in politics, and Wendell's only child was a girl. After we'd been married four years it looked like I wasn't going to give them a crown prince any time soon, so he and Cordelia decided to turn Carey into the royal heir. Wendell had already adopted him." Her eyes glinted. "And I wouldn't allow it. I made it clear that my son wasn't going to be railroaded into politics unless *he* wanted it. I think Cordelia would cheerfully have shot me. Things were never the same after that."

"And Carey's father? How involved was he in your son's life?"

Her face hardened. "He has nothing to do with Carey—Carey's never even met him. Leave him out of this."

"I can't promise the police will do that."

She laughed. "Please, Mr. MacLeod. Cordelia killed Wendell. I saw her with the gun. But she's Cordelia Spencer Sheehan and she's *connected.* Everyone in this state owes her favors. She isn't going to jail. She'll lie— hell, she already has—and they'll come after me."

"Don't you think you're being a little paranoid?"

"You don't know my mother-in-law. There's no such thing as being too paranoid where she's involved. Trust me on that. Cordelia is an amazing liar, Mr. MacLeod, and she's been around the block a few times in her life. Her husband was *governor,* for God's sake. Do you really think the district attorney is going to want to take on the Sheehan family? I'm sure she's already pulling strings, making calls. Evidence will be lost. Welcome to Louisiana politics, Mr. MacLeod. It's is a very ugly business."

"But won't being a Sheehan help you in the same way?"

"In Cordelia's mind, I am not a Sheehan—not by a long shot."

"Do you think any of your husband's political enemies could have killed him?"

"I told you, Cordelia killed him. But she doesn't hold all the cards this time out. This time, I hold the trumps, and today she and I are going to have a little chat."

She leaned back in her chair, smiling slyly.

"What do you mean?"

"She doesn't know yet, but when I drop my little bombshell, she'll stop telling the police and everyone else that I killed her precious son. After all those years of trying, he had to rape me to get me pregnant. And it's the long hoped for crown prince."

She got up out of her chair, walked over to the railing and leaned against it, facing me. "I'm carrying the last Sheehan son. I'm sure Cordelia won't want her grandchild born in prison. She's going to have to pin her crime on someone else. Things are going to be a lot different around here from now on."

My head was spinning. *Return the retainer and walk out of here, don't get involved with these people,* a voice whispered in of my head. But I, too, was caught in a trap not of my own making. If I dropped this case, whatever hold Cordelia had over Barbara would blow up in my face. I could lose my cushy job with Crown Oil. And Cordelia Spencer Sheehan undoubtedly had friends in Baton Rouge who could pull the necessary strings to get my license revoked. There wasn't any way I could get out of this case.

I stood up and offered Janna my hand across the table.

"Thank you, Mrs. Sheehan—Janna. If I have any other questions, I'll give you a call."

She took a card from her purse and slid it across the table, then shook my hand.

"Those are my cell and private phone numbers," she said. "Call anytime."

She went down the gazebo steps and along the walk to the back of the main house. The door shut behind her.

As I crossed the lawn, I reviewed what I knew. Janna wasn't telling me the whole truth, which meant she probably wasn't telling the police either. Shots fired, and she comes downstairs with a poker? That was almost as stupid as Cordelia picking up the gun. What was she hiding?

I walked around to the front of the house and stood there. The property was definitely a showplace. Surrounded by an eight-foot-high brick fence for privacy, the lot took up the entire block and was filled with gigantic live oaks. The house itself, a variation of the Greek-revival-style raised cottage with a double gallery at the front and a third floor with gables, faced the uptown side of the street. A fountain bubbled in the area delineated by the circular driveway, which ended in two electronic gates. I'd driven my own car through the gate to my right. It was still open, presumably so I could leave. On the other side of the fence, I could hear the traffic on St. Charles.

I opened the car door and hesitated. Something wasn't right.

I stood in the driveway. Wendell Sheehan's black Mercedes was there, presumably where he'd left it the night he died. I walked over to it and glanced up at the second floor of the house. The big windows on the right must be Janna's bedroom. Then it hit me.

Janna had said her room was at the top of the stairs. How on earth did Cordelia get to Wendell before Janna did, if they both came down almost immediately after hearing the shot? Even if Janna had stopped to call 911, she should have gotten to the first floor long before Cordelia. Cordelia claimed she'd looked in on both her grandchildren and only then come downstairs. Yet according to Janna, Cordelia was already in the drawing room when she got there, and she'd heard the second shot while she was on her way down.

What the hell had happened that night?

I pulled out my cell phone and dialed Janna's number. It switched immediately to voice mail. I hung up and tried the other number.

"Sheehan residence," a female voice answered.

"This is Chanse MacLeod, I just met with Mrs. Janna Sheehan." I made my voice as charming as possible. "May I speak with her, please? I forgot something I needed to ask her."

"Mrs. Sheehan is resting and asked not to be disturbed. I'll let her know you called."

The phone disconnected.

My job had just gotten a lot harder.

CHAPTER THREE

"THERE'S A STORM HEADING for the Gulf," Paige said casually as she unwrapped her po-boy from the grease-blotted butcher paper it had been wrapped in. She might just as well have said *It sure is humid this afternoon* and not the seven words nobody in New Orleans ever wanted to hear again. All of her attention was directed at the sandwich in her hands. She took a healthy bite, and mayonnaise squirted out the sides onto her fingers.

I was sitting in my easy chair, about to bite into my shrimp po-boy, my teeth just inches from the French bread. I put the po-boy down.

"You're not serious." I said.

Sweat formed in my armpits, and a numbness seemed to paralyze my brain for a moment. It was too soon, far too soon. Almost forty years had passed between Hurricanes Betsy and Katrina; surely we were entitled to another thirty-eight years before the next direct hit.

I didn't even want to think about evacuating again,

of packing what I could fit into my trunk and hitting the road for six weeks or even longer. Frantic questions raced through my mind. Would the levees hold? What if it came up the river this time the way Betsy had in the '60s? What if, what if, what if. A couple of mild hurricane seasons had made us all a little complacent.

Paige licked the mayonnaise from her fingers and smiled. "Ginevra is its name. Right now it's only Category 1, but once it hits the warm water in the Gulf . . ." She gave a halfhearted shrug as though to say *what can you do?* "Anyway, right now we're in the direct center of the cone of probability, for whatever that's worth." She took a healthy swig from her beer bottle. "Absolutely nothing, that's what it's worth. It's just a projection like always, and you know it can turn east or west. But people are starting to get nervous, which I guess isn't surprising." She made a face. "I really hate the term *cone of probability*. Why don't they just say the *sorry, you're fucked cone* and be done with it?"

I exhaled with relief, willing the stress out of my body. There wasn't any point getting upset or worried or freaking out yet.

"Are you saying I should start planning?" I asked. My fingers itched for a notepad to start making a list: *Change oil in car, get tires checked, figure out which way to go if I have to leave.*

She put her po-boy down and wiped mayonnaise off the sides of her mouth.

"Well, we don't want to wait till the last minute again, do we? The governor's office is in overdrive. They're probably going to declare a state of emergency tomorrow. City Hall is in a frenzy. Can you believe it? Maybe I'm cynical, but I'll bet you any amount of money they'll call for mandatory evacuation really early this time—and I'm leaving."

She took a swig from her beer.

Paige had still been working for the *Times-Picayune* when Katrina hit, and had stayed with a group of other reporters in Baton Rouge, coming into the city every day to report what was going on. She'd never talked to me about what she'd seen, saying only, "That's what I pay the shrink for." She'd written a book about the whole experience, and had even found an agent to help place it with a publisher, without luck. Paige had given up on it ever seeing print, and I knew she was disappointed. But whenever I brought it up she changed the subject.

She picked up the sandwich again and gave me a sideways look. "So, you had an audience with Her Majesty the Queen. What did you think of her?"

"What do *you* think about her?" I countered. "You've worked for her for almost a year now, and I'm sure you've got an opinion. You always do."

"Her Majesty never shows her face around the office," Paige said, grinning. "Get her oh-so-correct white gloves dirty? Really, Chanse, what are you thinking?"

She took another healthy bite of the po-boy, washing it down with another swig of beer. She hiccupped, and covered her mouth with her hand.

"Excuse me, sorry. Actually, Cordelia's not so bad. I covered a couple of the events for her foundation when

I was at the paper. She's very passionate about helping abused women, which makes me wonder about what her marriage was like. You know she didn't start all of that up until after her husband died. She's a horrible snob, of course, but she's been in or around politics her entire life and knows how to put on a good face for the hoi polloi—especially when she wants you to write a check. Then again, she could be much, much worse. She could do nothing for charity and just have lunch. I'm glad she does what she does—who'd do it if she didn't? Her shelters and foundation have done a lot of women a lot of good. What was your impression?"

She popped an errant shrimp into her mouth.

"I didn't like her. She has about as much charm as a rattlesnake. But then, I'm just the help."

Paige sipped her beer and frowned.

"And she wants you to look into Wendell's murder? It's a mess, you can be sure of that. Cordelia's fingerprints were the only ones on the gun, and she tested positive for powder blowback. If it were anyone else, she'd have been arrested already. But I can't imagine her killing her own son without a damned good reason. I guess it's just a matter of finding it. My sources in the police department—"

"Venus and Blaine?"

"You know I can't name my sources." She winked, crumpling up the greasy paper her sandwich had been wrapped in.

Venus Casanova and Blaine Tujague were friends of ours, and probably the two best detectives in the

NOPD. I'd met Venus during my time on the force. After I left, she took a dim view of my "interference" when our professional paths crossed. But over the years, our relationship had passed from dislike to grudging respect, and finally to friendship. I'd never been sure of her age, but she had two grown daughters who had married and settled in Memphis. She was tall, had been an athlete in college, and had kept her body fit. Her partner, Blaine, was in his early thirties, a Creole from a prominent society family that had no problem with his being gay but disapproved of his being a cop. He was a good-looking guy, about five-nine with bluish-black, curly hair, blue eyes, and thick muscles from hours spent at the gym. We'd become friends after joining the NOPD and for a time were fuck buddies. But that was ancient history. He lived with an older man now. Venus had stayed in their carriage house for a while after her house in New Orleans East had been destroyed by Katrina. A few months ago, she'd bought a house on General Pershing Street in Uptown. Paige and I had helped her move. Blaine and Venus became partners after her original partner retired and Blaine made detective grade. Surprisingly, their different styles meshed. They worked seamlessly together. Blaine also just happened to be the younger brother of Paige's boyfriend, Ryan.

"It was Janna's gun all right," Paige continued, "but her fingerprints weren't on it, even though she admitted using it at a firing range just a few days before the murder. Apparently, Cordelia is claiming that Janna killed

Wendell. *Someone* wiped Janna's fingerprints off that gun—Cordelia says it wasn't her. But why use Janna's gun if the killer wasn't planning to frame Janna? There are at least eight registered firearms in the Sheehan house. She had to know Janna wouldn't test positive for powder residue. It just doesn't make sense to me. My sources in the district attorney's office told me they aren't going to make an arrest until they're absolutely positive. A wrong move could be political suicide. The Sheehans are just too powerful."

Her mop of blonde-streaked red hair bounced as she shook her head.

"It's a juicy case, though. I almost wish I was back at the paper, so I could cover it."

"Did Venus and Blaine—er, your *sources*—fill you in on the statements the Sheehans gave?"

"Both Cordelia and Janna went downstairs after hearing a gunshot? They're either brave or really stupid. I would have called the police and waited upstairs until they arrived."

"Are you familiar with the layout of the house?"

Paige shook her head.

"This is *not* for publication," I warned.

She laughed. "Do you really think *Crescent City* is going to cover this story? I promise I won't say anything to anyone."

Paige always kept her word, so I continued.

"Janna's room is at the top of the stairs. The drawing room is at the bottom of the same staircase. I don't know where Cordelia's room is, but her story is, she heard the shot and checked on the kids, then went downstairs and saw Wendell's body. She said she went into shock, picked up the gun, and it went off a second time."

"With you so far."

"Janna's story is, she heard the shot, called 911, and was on the stairs when she heard the second shot. Cordelia is in her seventies, at the very least. I'll give you that she is pretty spry, but how did she hear the shot, check in on both her grandchildren, and still manage to get downstairs before Janna when all Janna did was call 911? And why didn't Cordelia check on Janna before she went downstairs? Even if she hates her daughter-in-law, and I'll stipulate to that, don't you think she would have checked on her?"

"The plot thickens. What did they have to say when you pointed that out?"

"That's just it. I didn't know the layout of the house until I was leaving there this morning. And now neither one of them will take my calls, or call me back. I think I'm being played. I just can't figure out why. Cordelia made it quite clear that I'm not to focus on her family."

I took a swig of my own beer.

"Isn't Loren McKeithen representing Cordelia? Why don't you call him? I know you think he fucked you over the last time you dealt with him, but you are working for Cordelia too—and if he hasn't caught this discrepancy yet, telling him is one way to earn your pay."

That was something, I admitted. "Did you ever meet Janna?"

"I know Janna. Not well, but I've met her a few times

at company parties and things like that. She was perfectly nice to me. I liked her and felt sorry for her. Wendell was horrible to her. If I were Janna I'd have capped his ass years ago. Before he stepped down as publisher to run for the Senate, he used to come back from lunch tanked. Fridays he'd go to Galatoire's and not return. I often wondered how he thought he could get elected. Then again, it's not like we Louisianans look down on drinking. And he did okay in the state legislature, and on the City Council. I guess the Sheehan name still carries a lot of weight. "

"How was he horrible to her? Do you think there was abuse?"

"That would be weird, given Cordelia's work. He was very abrupt to her, but I didn't see any evidence of physical abuse. I remember at the Christmas party last year—he just ignored her and never introduced her to anyone, either. The first time I met her was right after I was hired; they had a party so everyone could meet the new editor. You know, one of those things I hate going to and avoid like the plague if I can. He introduced me to everyone except Janna. I about fell through the floor when I introduced myself at the bar and she told me her name." She tapped her index finger on her chin. "Wendell was kind of a pig. Always saying inappropriate things to women, touching us—never anything that truly crossed the line, I'd have knocked a few of his teeth loose if he had—but you know what I mean. Putting his arm around our shoulders, touching on the arms. That sort of thing. He thought he was God's gift to women."

"What about Monica Davis? Did you know her?"

"You've already heard that story? Take it from me, it's just that—a story. Monica *hated* Wendell."

"I heard she was—"

"That was ancient history, Chanse. Trust me, there was no way in hell Monica would have started it up again. Was it Janna who said—"

I cut her off. "No, it wasn't. Was Wendell well liked around the company?"

"Not really. I mean, he was the boss, and could—and did—fire people at will."

"Anyone who might hold a grudge?"

"Who likes to be fired? But Wendell stepped down from the company months ago. I doubt anyone would have harbored a grudge all this time and waited. You get fired, you want payback right then and there."

"Who took over when Wendell stepped down?"

"Rachel Sheehan. She's married to Wendell's cousin Quentin. Rachel was assistant publisher and moved right into his office. She's a lot easier to deal with than Wendell—she's tough, but she's fair and doesn't expect the impossible. Wendell did at times. Her maiden name was Delesdernier. Sound familiar?"

Paige watched my blank face and laughed.

"For God's sake, Chanse, you are so fucking oblivious at times. Rachel's father was mayor when Wendell's father was governor. They fought almost constantly. They were bitter enemies."

"And his daughter married Governor Sheehan's nephew?" That was interesting.

"I always figured it was a political marriage—you know, the Delesdernier machine marrying the Sheehan machine. As much as we like to think marriages aren't mergers nowadays, it still happens. Cordelia's marriage was a merger, after all. Bobby Sheehan's father was mayor, he built up a pretty strong machine here in New Orleans, but they were upstarts. The Spencer machine had been around since before the Civil War. Cordelia was the last Spencer. When they married, the two machines merged."

"I was under the impression that Rachel and Wendell didn't get along. Janna said that she and Quentin moved out because of it. How did they work together?"

"The friction wasn't between Rachel and Wendell—it was between Quentin and Wendell. *They* couldn't stand each other. Rachel was really happy when Quentin decided to leave the Sheehan compound. I think they got a place in the Marigny."

I made a mental note to bump Quentin up on my interview list.

"What does Quentin do?"

"He lives off the trust." Paige held up her hand. "Don't ask me to explain it, because I can't. Everything—the house, the company, all of it—belongs to the trust, and Cordelia is the trustee. All the Sheehans have an income from the trust, but for anything more than that they have to get Cordelia's permission—and I don't think she gives it very often. Apparently, she likes controlling them."

I smirked. "It seems so out of character for her."

Paige laughed. "I believe the terms of the trust were part of the problem. Quentin didn't think he should have to ask Cordelia for his money—and I can't say that I blame him. Wendell couldn't have liked it, either. Can you imagine having to go to your mother for everything?"

Her face froze for a moment.

"I'm sorry, Chanse. How is your mother doing? I should have asked when I got here."

"It's all right, really." What was there to say? "She's in good hands. She seems to be responding to the treatments she's getting, and it looks pretty good right now. The doctors are cautiously optimistic, but there are no guarantees. You know."

I changed the subject.

"You don't think any of Wendell's political enemies might be behind this, do you?" I finally said before we both started to squirm in our seats.

"I don't see how." Paige said tentatively, taking her cue from me. "It was Janna's gun. Cordelia fired it. Besides the kids, they were the only people in the house that night. That's all there is to it, Chanse. But check with his campaign manager, Stephen Robideaux. He'd know. He came down from Lafayette to run the campaign. The office is actually only a few blocks from here, on St. Charles between Euterpe and Melpomene. You know which one I mean? I think it used to be a dress shop before the flood."

"I think I do." I wrote his name down in my pad. "Thanks, Paige."

"Just be careful, Chanse. The Sheehans aren't people you want to mess around with. Talk to Loren about the discrepancy in their statements—don't go sticking your nose in where they don't want it, if you know what I mean."

She glanced at her watch.

"I am out of here. Ryan's on his way back from the North Shore."

She gave me a hug. "I'm sorry I'm not around as much, and sorry again about having to cancel last night. I really miss you."

"I miss you, too."

I walked her to her car and stood on the curb until she drove away. I was just about to go back into the house when I turned to watch Paige's retreat and noticed a car on the Coliseum Square side of the street. That was odd. Most people parked on the opposite side, in front of the houses. Paige's headlights hit the parked car, revealing two people sitting inside it. I got a brief glimpse before she drove past them.

I stood there for a moment, squinting through the gloom, trying to get a better look. It was a midsize car, maybe a Toyota Corolla or a Honda Accord. There was not enough light to get an idea of the color, other than it was something dark, maybe green or blue or black. It was parked just outside the pyramid of light cascading down from a streetlamp, and not quite obscured from my line of vision by one of the massive live oaks in the park. I felt a rush of adrenaline.

It's probably nothing, I told myself, *probably just some-one waiting for someone to get home over on that side. You're overreacting. Whoever they are, it's got nothing to do with you.*

Nevertheless, I went inside and closed and locked the door, then retrieved my pistol from my bottom desk drawer. I checked to see that it was loaded. I parted the blinds on the door and looked across the park. I was just about to open the door when the car's engine started, the headlights came on, and it headed down Coliseum.

I turned the deadbolt closed and put the gun back in the drawer.

You're being paranoid, I told myself. *Relax. There's no reason for anyone to be spying on you.*

But my instincts were telling me the exact opposite.

I shook it off and sat down at my desk. I retrieved Loren's business card from my Rolodex, called his cell phone and got his voice mail, which was irritat-ing. I was tired of leaving messages for people. "Loren, Chanse MacLeod here," I said. "I've interviewed both Mrs. Sheehans and there's a serious discrepancy in their stories. We need to talk. Call me."

I spent the rest of the evening reading Abby's report on the Sheehans. Abby was my research assistant. She loved doing research, and was good at ferreting out in-formation it would have taken me days to find. I found myself relying on her more and more.

By the time I went to bed a few hours later, I was an expert on the Sheehan family history. Most of it was incredibly dull and probably had nothing to do with the case at hand, but it was good to have all the background. Before I undressed, I checked through the blinds in the front window to be sure the car wasn't there. It wasn't. I felt oddly relieved, and cursed myself for a fool. But I went ahead anyway and double-checked all my doors before I climbed into bed. Better safe than sorry.

The next morning I drank a pot of coffee and showered before walking the three blocks from my apartment to St. Charles Avenue. Even though it was only ten in the morning, the sun was blasting the city and it was already over ninety degrees. I was soaked with sweat by the time I made it to the Avenue. A streetcar clacked past on its way downtown. I mopped my forehead with the front of my Polo shirt.

Wendell Sheehan's campaign office was located in a small enclave of businesses. There were campaign posters in the window, with an interesting slogan: *Sheehan for a new Louisiana.* Well, I reflected as I pushed the door open, the old Louisiana did leave a lot to be desired.

The interior was lit with fluorescent tubes, and there were desks going all the way back to the rear wall, with boxes piled everywhere. Apart from a young man standing at a desk about halfway to the rear of the office, packing files into a large box, the place was completely deserted.

"May I help you?" he asked, with a smile that lit up his face and a mouth full of straight white teeth with a slight underbite that made his lower lip stick out a bit. He was good-looking, probably in his mid-twenties, maybe five-foot-seven or -eight, with a compact yet strong build. A red Polo shirt hugged his chest and shoulders. His low-rise jeans were almost worn through at the knees. He had dark skin and curly light brown hair.

"I'm looking for Stephen Robideaux," I said, shivering slightly in the air-conditioning as I walked back to where he was standing. Up close, he looked even better.

"Stephen's at a meeting. He should be back in about an hour or so."

He resumed placing files in the box.

"I gather you're closing down the office."

"Not much point in having a campaign office for a dead candidate, is there?" he said. "It's a shame, too. Wendell was the only candidate who gave a shit about gay rights. What are we going to do now? We'll wind up with some moderate Democrat who anywhere else would be considered a Republican." He slammed the lid down on the box. "Or even worse, that prick from Metairie will get re-elected. That would be a disaster for the state, an absolute disaster." He stopped and smiled ruefully. "Sorry, I've gotten kind of passionate about politics. My name's Rory."

He stuck his hand out. His grip was strong.

"Chanse MacLeod. And don't worry about the politics thing. Since Katrina, I've taken a bigger interest myself. So, what are you going to do now that the campaign is over?"

"I have another job." He gave me his million-dollar smile. "I was just a volunteer. I came in on Monday nights and all day on Wednesdays. I'm here today to help close up the office and clean my stuff out of the desk I was using. Apparently, I'm the only one. Probably I'll just volunteer for the presidential race this year, and if the party finds someone as good as Wendell, I'll work for him or her."

"Did you know Wendell well?"

"His cousin is married to my sister. A lot of people here thought I was volunteering because of the family connection, but I really believed in Wendell. I believed in the changes he wanted to make for the country and for the state. I wouldn't have been here if he was one of those wing-nut politicians. I thought he could go all the way to the White House."

"Your sister would be Rachel Sheehan?"

"How did you know?"

"What exactly did Wendell stand for, anyway?" I asked, deflecting the question.

"Equal rights for all Americans. Rebuilding the wetlands to reduce storm surges from future hurricanes. Category 5 levee protection for New Orleans. Health care reform and access to affordable health care for everyone. More money for public education. Ending the wars."

"Sounds good to me."

Rory grabbed an empty box off the floor and began placing files from another drawer into it.

"It sounded good to a lot of people. Wendell would have won the election, you know. A lot of people thought we couldn't have both senators be from New Orleans, but we were going to make history."

"Did he have a lot of political enemies?"

"Of course he did." He gave me a wary look. "You don't think—? Who are you, anyway?"

"I work for the family," I said. I opened my wallet and passed him one of my business cards. "I've been hired by Cordelia Sheehan to look into the murder."

"Wow." He sat down in a worn rolling chair and leaned back. "I don't think I've ever met an honest-to-goodness private detective before. I talked to the police detectives yesterday. They didn't say anything about his political enemies, though. Wendell got death threats all the time, mostly from right-wing nut-jobs—you know, the ones who think life begins at conception, that anyone who isn't white can't be an American—and sadly, there are plenty of those in Louisiana. Stephen turned those all over to the police yesterday. We kept copies. We gave the originals to the FBI every time one came in. But I'd have to say that, as ugly as politics can be, I don't think anyone would stoop to murder to get rid of a candidate—at least not the way this was done."

"You only came in twice a week?"

"It depended on when I was needed. I have a full-time job and I'm in the master's program at Tulane, studying political science. I got credit for working on the campaign."

"Anything unusual you noticed going on lately?"

He thought about it for a moment. He really was attractive. I wondered if he was gay or just progressive—it was hard to tell, these days.

"The only thing that struck me as weird was this other volunteer, Dave Zeringue, a nice guy who came in a few times to stuff envelopes. A closet case, if ever there was one."

"Was that what was weird about him?"

"Well, no. He—" Rory hesitated. "He didn't seem to fit in. There was nothing concrete about it, it was just a feeling I had. I mean, whenever we would talk about issues—and that was practically all the time—he seemed uncomfortable with our positions. It wasn't anything he said. He never really contributed an opinion to discussions, if you know what I mean. I just got the sense that he wasn't one of us, and I couldn't quite figure out why he was volunteering for Wendell Sheehan. Last week he didn't show, and Stephen asked me to call him. His cell phone was disconnected, and the landline information he gave us was a wrong number. Like I said, nothing major. You asked about weird stuff."

He gave me that big smile again. I made a note of the name.

"Were you here on Monday night, by any chance?"

"Me and a couple of other volunteers. We were making cold calls for donations. Wendell and Stephen were in the back office the whole time." He gestured over his shoulder at the door in the back wall. "Wendell came out and thanked us all for helping. He shook everyone's hand, told us how we were going to make a difference, and then he left."

"What time was that?"

"I didn't really notice. I left at nine, and it was well before that. Maybe a little before eight? I wasn't paying attention. I was trying to focus on what I was doing."

"Do you know where Wendell was going when he left?" According to the two Mrs. Sheehans, he hadn't got home until eleven-thirty. That leaves about three-and-a-half hours unaccounted for.

"He didn't say. I assumed he went to the Delacroix. He always ate there on Mondays. He raved about the food there."

The Delacroix was a small bar and restaurant on St. Charles Avenue. I made a note to stop by and talk to the staff.

"Had he been drinking?"

"Of course not!" He seemed shocked. "I never saw him take a drink."

I was about to ask him another question when my cell phone rang. I excused myself and stepped outside to take the call.

"What's up, Abby?"

"I've been out in Kenner following a lead." I could hear traffic in the background. "I'm heading back into the city. You need to buy me lunch."

Whenever Abby turned up something good, she demanded I buy her a meal.

"What kind of lead?"

She sighed in exasperation. "Did you or did you not

ask me to look into Barbara's past? I found some really juicy stuff. You going to buy me lunch, or would you rather wait for me to write up the report?"

I checked my watch. It was almost eleven.

"How long before you get to the St. Charles exit?"

"Ten minutes, tops." She had the decency to move the phone away from her mouth before she screamed, *"Stupid motherfucker! That's why you have a turn signal, asshole!"* She brought the phone back to her mouth. "Sorry about that."

"It's okay." I said. "Why don't you meet me at Slice?"

Slice was an Italian joint across the street from the campaign office.

"Will do."

She hung up. I walked back into the office, where Rory had resumed packing files. He really was cute.

"I have an appointment, so I can't wait for Stephen any longer," I told him. "Can you give him my card and have him call me?"

"Sure." He smiled.

"And if you think of anything else out of the ordinary, no matter how small or inconsequential it might seem to you, will you let me know?"

He nodded.

When I got to the door, I remembered the question I'd been about to ask when Abby called.

"Rory?"

"Uh-huh." He didn't look up from what he was doing.

"You said you never saw Wendell take a drink?"

"No. When his first wife died, he began drinking a

lot, and it became a problem, so he joined AA. He was very open about it, actually."

Janna had insisted he was drunk on Monday night. She'd said he came home drunk all the time. If he had gone to the Delacroix, maybe he had a few drinks there.

"Thank you, Rory. One more thing."

He looked up.

"Did he seem different that night? Worried? Preoccupied about something?"

He thought for a minute.

"Not that I noticed. He seemed the way he always did. Sorry. I should have paid more attention."

"Thanks again," I said, and walked out into the heat.

CHAPTER FOUR

I DIDN'T HAVE TO wait long for Abby.

I'd taken a table right inside the front door, and had just enough time to order a Coke when I saw the wreck of an Oldsmobile she shared with her boyfriend, Jephtha, shoot past on St. Charles. I couldn't help but grin. The car was a disaster. It was almost twenty years old, with a cracked windshield and dents all over it. The driver's side rearview mirror was missing, and at some point it had been painted with defective paint. It looked like it had the mange. Jephtha had inherited the car from his grandmother, along with her house in the Irish Channel. Despite looking like it would fall apart if you breathed on it, the car ran extremely well. Less than five minutes later Abby walked through the front door.

Abby was a pretty girl. Originally from Plaquemines Parish, she'd moved to New Orleans after the flood and started dancing at the Catbox Club on Bourbon Street. That was where she'd met Jephtha, who had a weakness for erotic dancers. They were both in their early twenties. Jephtha was a computer whiz with a criminal record whom I kept on retainer; he could literally hack his way into any system. If I needed information and didn't really care if it was obtained legally, I put Jephtha on it. Abby danced to pay her way through the University of New Orleans's pre-law program, where she was one semester away from graduating. She was hoping to get into the Tulane Law School once she finished. When I'd asked her to help me with some research, she was so fast and efficient at it that I'd encouraged her to get certified as a private eye. She was a godsend. She loved doing all the tedious things that bored me, and I was more than happy to farm them out to her. She enjoyed tinkering with disguises. She'd done theater in high school, and had taken a course at UNO in stage makeup. Several times she'd shown up on my doorstep in a disguise and I hadn't recognized her. She was dressed to impress today, wearing a nice pair of navy blue slacks beneath a red silk shirt, exposing a tantalizing glimpse of her impressive cleavage. Her hair was all one color for a change, dark brown.

I'd had reservations about working with someone, having got used to toiling along by myself since leaving the police force. She had obliterated those reservations in no time. The whole arrangement was going so well I was beginning to dread the day she decided to go out on her own. She was a natural snoop. Plus, she could always make me laugh. She gave me an impish grin as she slid into the chair across from me.

"This wig is driving me crazy," she said. "It's too fucking hot for wigs. Besides, you haven't even seen the new color I just changed it to. Reddish with blonde streaks." She winked. "Like Paige."

"So why cover it up with a wig?" I had to ask.

She had a lot of them. She'd explained to me once that wearing wigs was easier than dying her hair. She'd added with a lascivious grin, "It gives the spenders at the Catbox Club the illusion of a different girl, to spice things up a bit and loosen their wallets." She made a lot of money dancing there.

"I was interviewing a retired police detective, and I didn't think he'd take me seriously if I showed up looking like a stripper," she explained. "I was torn between professional lady detective and innocent young girl, but I decided to go with professional woman. After all, I don't get too many chances to wear this outfit. And this brown hair goes well with it, don't you think? More so than the red."

She blotted her forehead with her napkin as our waitress materialized. Abby ordered a Coke and two slices of pepperoni pizza. I ordered the same, figuring I could work off the trans fat at the gym, and waited until the waitress left before speaking again.

"A retired police detective? What are you on to?"

She placed her elbows on the table and rested her chin on her fists, beaming at me.

"Ah, Chanse. I am so good at my job. You should give me a raise."

She always asked for a raise when she'd gotten her hands on something good—and it was amazing how Abby always came up with good stuff.

"I'll take it under advisement."

The waitress placed Abby's Coke in front of her. She took a big swallow, and waited until we were alone.

"I'll start at the beginning. First of all, there wasn't anything interesting in Barbara's background before she married Roger Palmer. Born and raised on the West Bank, went to UNO and dropped out. She met Roger at an opening at the art gallery where she worked. They had a rather whirlwind courtship. Did you know Roger Palmer was significantly older than Barbara?"

"I knew there was an age difference, but not how much."

Barbara had mentioned it a few times, on the rare occasions when she talked about her first husband. I'd never given it much thought. Young women marry rich old men all the time. It was practically a cliché. For that matter, Wendell Sheehan had about twenty years on Janna.

"Barbara was all of twenty-five when she married him. He was in his mid-fifties, what was politely called a 'confirmed bachelor.' What does that tell you?"

Confirmed bachelor was old New Orleans society code for homosexual. It wasn't always true, but it was the way polite society acknowledged it without actually saying so.

"Barbara married a gay man. Interesting."

It certainly explained why she'd never had any problems with my sexuality.

"That's what I thought, too." She took another sip of her Coke. "Different strokes and all that. Whatever the reasons were—which we'll never know—they got married. Roger had never been linked to another woman, at least none that I could find. And four years later, Roger died and left Barbara everything. The house, his money, everything."

"What's so unusual about that? Under Louisiana's Napoleonic Code she would have gotten half of everything, whether he wanted her to have it or not."

"Roger didn't die peacefully in his bed, Chanse."

"How did he die?"

"He broke his neck falling down a flight of stairs in his house. The story Barbara gave out was that she was at a big fundraising party and came home to find him dead. There were only two problems: no one at the fundraiser remembered seeing Barbara there, and she was having an affair on the side. The cops never could find any hard evidence that she was unfaithful, but tongues were wagging in the Garden District."

"And who was she supposed to be having an affair with?"

Abby licked her lips.

"This is where it gets really good. Wendell Sheehan."

"Are you serious?"

"According to the gossips, it had been going on for several years, but it wasn't like anyone had pictures to prove it. I should charge you combat pay. You have no idea how tedious it is going through all of those old society pages, even if it is fun to read between the lines."

Abby slurped down more Coke.

"Let me backtrack a bit. The accounts made it pretty

clear that the police thought foul play was involved in Roger's death. It was all over the papers for two or three days. When the coroner's report came back with a judgment of accidental death, the case was officially closed."

"And?"

"It didn't smell right to me, so I tracked down the lead detective on the case. That's what I was doing in Kenner this morning. This guy—Archie Barousse—was just happy to have someone to talk to, poor thing. His wife died a couple of years ago, and his kids all moved away. Retired cops are really nice, you know?"

"I'm sure it didn't hurt to have an attractive young woman with her shirt unbuttoned asking questions."

Abby looked down, and sheepishly corrected the situation.

"Anyway, he believes that Roger Palmer was murdered, and it was covered up. The mayor ordered him to close the case *before* the coroner's report came back, and talk around the station was that the pressure on Mayor Delesdernier came from Baton Rouge. Archie is still bitter about his investigation being shut down before it got started."

She leaned across the table.

"And who was in the governor's mansion then? That would be none other than the sainted Bobby Sheehan— Wendell Sheehan's father."

"But Bobby Sheehan and Gaston Delesdernier were enemies. He wouldn't have done Sheehan any favors— nor his family."

"You think it's all just a bunch of coincidences?

Let's see." She started ticking things off on her fingers. "Roger Palmer dies in a 'fall' down the stairs. His much younger wife is rumored to be having an affair with the governor's son. The mayor himself orders the investigation closed, under pressure from the governor. And did I mention that five months after Roger Palmer died, his young widow gave birth to a daughter? They were *politicians*, Chanse. They probably traded favors. *You close this investigation and I'll give you this.* That's how things get done in this state.

"This is what I think. Wendell knocked up Barbara and Barbara was afraid Roger would show her the front door when he found out. He became *inconvenient*, and shortly thereafter he was dead. Under mysterious circumstances."

"It's an interesting theory, but there are no facts."

I found it hard to believe Barbara might have killed her husband. Maybe I just didn't want to believe it. Barbara never talked about her daughter, Brenda. I heard Barbara's voice in my head: *I owe her.*

"It's circumstantial, to be sure," Abby said, "but *poor* people who don't have friends in the governor's mansion get convicted on a lot less than that every day. Anyway, there's your connection between Barbara and the Sheehans. It was the only thing I could come up with, outside of some associations between Barbara and Cordelia on charity committees and so forth. There's nothing I can find that would warrant Barbara owing them a big debt of gratitude. Not on the scale of helping her cover up a murder."

She finished her second slice of pizza and leaned back in her chair.

"Alleged murder." I corrected her. "Nice work, Abby. Type up a report for the file and e-mail it to me."

"How's the Sheehan case coming? Need me to do anything?"

"There is something. According to a volunteer at the campaign office, Wendell had dinner at the Delacroix every Monday night. Can you talk to the staff? See if he was there the night he died? Find out if he ate dinner alone or if he had company. And if he had anything to drink."

She scribbled notes. "I'll get a photo of him off the web. Anything else?"

"The two Mrs. Sheehans have been lying to me—and probably to the police. According to his campaign worker, Wendell left the office a good three-and-a-half hours before Janna and Cordelia say he got home. Janna said that he was drunk when he came in, that he drank all the time, he was drunk when he sprained her wrist and raped her. The volunteer said that Wendell was in recovery and going to AA meetings."

"Alcoholics fall off the wagon all the time, Chanse. But it's weird how similar this case is to Roger Palmer's. Two wealthy and powerful men married to younger women who aren't from the same class, both men die mysteriously when their wives are pregnant. It's like Roger Palmer's death was the blueprint for Wendell's—except for how the murder was committed, of course."

"If Cordelia was involved in the cover-up of Roger Palmer's murder, why *not* use the same setup for her son?" I said. "Who'd remember after all this time? Why all the nonsense with Janna's gun?"

Abby finished her Coke and signaled the waitress for another.

"Think about it, Chanse. Suppose it wasn't premeditated. Even if Wendell ate dinner at the Delacroix like he always did, how long would that take? An hour? Two, tops? There's still a lot of time unaccounted for that night. Who's to say what went on in those hours before the gun was fired? The only people who know are Cordelia and Janna—and Wendell, but he's not talking any time soon—and they're doing their little finger-pointing shtick. It's really not a bad legal strategy. Unless one of them confesses, who knows which one really did it?"

"But Cordelia ordered me to find other suspects, to spare the family name."

"Suppose what Janna said about Wendell was true," Abby said. "Suppose he did rough her up every now and then when he was drinking. Wendell has dinner and then goes straight home from the office. He starts to drink. And the more he drinks, the more abusive he gets, till Janna shoots him in self-defense. But she's also pregnant. The last thing in the world Cordelia wants is for her grandson to be born in jail. So the two of them come up with a story on the quick. Cordelia wipes the gun, then fires it into the floor to make her story seem right."

"Janna tested negative for residue," I countered.

"Please. Anyone who watches *CSI* or *Law and Order* knows all you have to do is wash your hands in bleach to get rid of that—and the crime lab never tests hands for bleach. That's why their stories don't work. They had to think fast, and it was the best they could come up with. They had to call 911, the kids were in the house— Any chance of talking to them?"

"The women aren't taking my calls, and anyway I doubt they'd let me talk to the kids."

"You can't *not* talk to them, Chanse. If someone else killed Wendell, that someone had to be in the house. There's your pretext, to see if they noticed or saw anything out of the ordinary."

"Maybe I *should* give you a raise," I said. "You know, we only have their word for it they hated each other."

Perhaps there was some friction in the beginning— there was no doubt in my mind Cordelia wouldn't have wanted Wendell to marry Janna. But in the years since then, they'd lived together in the same house. They'd had to tolerate each other. Was it impossible to believe they could have become friends? Or if not friends, allies? Janna was stepmother to Cordelia's only grandchild, and Janna's son was being raised under Cordelia's roof. And now Janna was pregnant with Cordelia's grandson.

If Wendell was drinking, and violent—there'd be a medical record somewhere of Janna's sprained wrist to backup her story—it wasn't a stretch to think he could have become a danger to Janna's unborn child. From there, it wasn't hard to conclude that one of the two Mrs. Sheehans killed him to protect the baby, and concocted their ridiculous, contradictory stories to cloud the issue. I only had Janna's word that she'd told no one about the pregnancy. If Cordelia knew—if Wendell came home and got violent with Janna—would Cordelia have killed her son to save her grandchild?

I knew the answer to that—a resounding *hell yes*.

"We have to retrace Wendell's steps that night," I told Abby.

"What do you need me to do, boss?"

She whipped out her Blackberry.

"Talk to Wendell's friends and associates. Find out if he went to the Delacroix that night. See if anyone there heard or saw anything. See if he went anywhere else before going home. And find out what his state of mind was. This is a long shot, but see if you can find out who Carey Sheehan's father was. Janna wouldn't tell me, and I asked her twice—she reacted vehemently, insisting he had nothing to do with Carey and nothing to do with her."

"The lady doth protest too much?"

"Something like that. Maybe she was having an affair, the way Barbara was. Might as well see if everything in these two cases is parallel."

Her fingers flew over the tiny keyboard. She glanced up.

"You really need to get one of these instead of that tired old phone you use. Anything else?"

"We need to talk to Carey and Alais Sheehan. They were both in the house that night. Alais isn't returning to college this semester. She goes to Ole Miss. See what you can dig up on her. Carey had swim practice yesterday. Maybe you could catch him there. May I recommend your schoolgirl look? He's only thirteen, and hormonal."

"You aren't suggesting I take advantage of a child, are you? That's sick."

"I didn't say *sleep* with him. Lift your mind out of the gutter. Isn't your specialty getting information from men?"

She closed her Blackberry.

"He's a boy, which is like shooting fish in a barrel. And my specialty is getting *money* from men."

She slipped the phone into her purse and stood up.

"I'm off. I'll get that report to you this afternoon, and e-mail a progress report to you tonight. Thanks for lunch, Chanse. Can I give you a lift home?"

"I have to stop by Wendell's office and see if his campaign manager is back yet."

I put two twenties into the little tray the waitress had discreetly slipped onto our table, and stood up.

"I take it you're not dancing tonight? No class, either?"

"I took the week off. Makes the regulars tip more when you come back. Why do you ask?"

We walked out into the blinding heat.

"There was a car parked on the other side of Coliseum Square from my place last night. Someone was just sitting there. It may have been nothing, but if the car's there tonight, it wouldn't hurt to check it out."

Her face lit up. She loved doing surveillance.

"Give me a call if it's there. Should be a piece of cake. I'll bring the dogs. No one would suspect a girl walking her dogs, right?"

I couldn't help grinning as I watched her walk away.

A little more experience under her belt and she was going to be the best private eye in Louisiana. Maybe I should make her a partner.

The only person in Wendell's campaign office now was a short, stocky man with reddish-blond hair and a red face wet with sweat, talking into his cell phone. His blue button-down shirt was soaked at the armpits. He waved me into a seat by his desk, looking apologetic. I listened to his end of the call.

"Uh-huh . . . yes, I know . . . there's got to be another viable candidate somewhere in the state . . . I always said it was unlikely we'd have both senators from New Orleans . . . it's never happened before and you know how those Baptists in North Louisiana are. They hate everything about South Louisiana . . . they hate Catholics and think New Orleans is Sodom and Gomorrah all over again . . . I know . . . a Sheehan would have had the best shot, especially with Cordelia campaigning. She's only a little less popular than the Virgin Mary . . . All right . . . I have someone here. I'll call you later."

He flipped his phone closed and smiled weakly.

"Sorry about that. How can I help you?"

"Are you Stephen Robideaux?"

"I am."

He stuck his hand out. It was warm and moist and soft. I gave it a brief grasp and shake, letting go as soon as I politely could, resisting the urge to wipe my hand on my pants leg.

"Chanse MacLeod. I stopped by earlier. I've been hired by Cordelia Sheehan to look into her son's death."

"Rory told me. I have your card here somewhere." He gestured at the top of his desk, a scattered, disorganized mess, and gave me a sheepish smile. "I was going to call. Anything I can do to help the Sheehans, you can count me in."

"Do you mind answering some questions?"

"Fire away." His face went white. "I'm sorry, that was in poor taste, given the circumstances."

"Rory told me you came down from Lafayette to run Wendell's campaign?"

"More or less. I worked for the state party for a long time, and I run a consulting business for political campaigns. I've helped elect quite a few Democrats to Baton Rouge. But this was my first campaign for a national office. In fact, I was the one who convinced Wendell to run in the first place."

He seemed proud of himself, a little pompous, like he was trying to impress me.

"Really? How did that come about?"

"When his first wife died and he retired from public life, it was a loss for the entire state. Wendell was a rising star, and with the Sheehan and Spencer names behind him there would have been no stopping him. He was attorney general, remember, and the state party was prepping him for a run at the governor's mansion. Next it could have been the White House. You never know."

He removed his glasses and rubbed his eyes. "But his wife's death devastated him. He backed away from everything and focused on running the family business and raising his daughter. I thought maybe when he re-married he'd return to politics, but no."

"He ran for mayor." I pointed out.

"The hurricane and what happened after woke a lot of us up. Wendell realized that Louisiana—and the country—lacked leadership. He saw the direction the country had been going in while he wasn't involved, and he didn't like it. Actually, he *hated* it. So he ran for mayor."

"I voted for him." I said.

"As long as I live I will never understand the outcome of that election. Maybe there were shenanigans involved—it wouldn't be the first time that's happened in New Orleans. But Wendell decided he could do more good for New Orleans, and Louisiana, in the Senate. After the scandal about the incumbent and his penchant for prostitutes, I came down to meet with him. It wasn't hard to convince him to run for that seat. We were getting support like you wouldn't believe, from all over the state. The Sheehan name was like money in the bank—or ballots in the box, if you'll forgive me. Granted, the election is still two years away, but by the time it truly geared up we would have had an unbeatable machine put together."

"Do you think political enemies could have done this? Someone who didn't want him in the Senate?"

"I seriously doubt it. Murder isn't their style. They prefer slander and innuendo. Not that they were in a position to throw stones. I was really looking forward to doing rebuttal ads to whatever they threw at us. There was no viable opponent for the primary; all the primary drama is going to be on the other side, and I don't think even they would go as far as murder. This whole thing is such a mess. Do the police really think Cordelia could have shot him? I find that so hard to believe. It's just not like her."

"I'm not privy to the police investigation, so I can't answer that. But she fired the gun, and hers were the only fingerprints on it."

"I'm sure there's another explanation."

"You were here the night of the murder?"

"Wendell and I met with some potential donors, and then we came here to make calls. He was in a really good mood. He left around eight."

"Did he say where he was going?"

"No. I assumed he was going home."

"Did you notice anything odd in the days before? Did he seem worried, or upset about anything?"

"Wendell was the consummate politician, always smiling, always cheerful, always in a good mood. He never let anyone see what he was really feeling. To be honest, I didn't really know him that well. All we ever talked about was politics, the state of the country, strategy, what he wanted to do when he got to the Senate."

"And how did things seem between Wendell and his wife?"

"I couldn't have picked a better wife for a candidate."

This was the first time anyone had said something positive about Janna.

"Really? I was under the impression she was a liability to him."

"Not at all. Wendell was Louisiana aristocracy, born to privilege and power. So of course he'd be called an elitist. But his wife was young, beautiful, smart, engaging, with a charisma all her own. She was brought up poor, went to public schools. The bastard son could have been a problem, but when you balance that against an opponent who goes to prostitutes, it didn't seem like such a big deal. And while Wendell was pro-choice, the fact that his wife chose to keep her baby instead of having an abortion was something we could work with. It made her even more appealing to voters. She could talk about what she went through, her decision to have the baby. Wendell was perfect. Janna was perfect. And with Cordelia out there campaigning—she's part of what we call the Holy Trinity, along with Lindy Boggs and Marjorie Morrison—the Republicans wouldn't have had a chance."

"How did Wendell feel about Janna being involved in the campaign?"

"At first he was worried about how she'd do, how she would handle the pressure. I met with her a few times, and talked to her. She's very bright, and learns fast. I like her a lot. We did a luncheon up in Baton Rouge where she spoke to the League of Women Voters. They would have elected *her.* After that, Wendell had no doubts about her."

"Did they seem happily married?"

"I don't know what went on when they were in private, but publicly they were a happy, loving couple."

"What about his friends, the people he hung out with and confided in?"

"I don't think he really had a lot of close friends. He knew a lot of people, but I don't think you could call them friends." Stephen shook his head. "I can't help you there."

"And you have no idea where he might have gone when he left here on Monday night?"

"Not if he didn't go straight home."

His cell phone rang, a tinkling version of Alice Cooper's old hit "Elected." He looked at it. "I have to take this. Do you mind?"

I offered him my hand. "Thank you."

"Anything I can do to help, just let me know."

"One last thing. Do you know how his first wife died?"

"She fell down the stairs and broke her neck. A terrible tragedy."

He answered the phone.

I waved and walked out into the sunshine. Within seconds I was drenched in sweat. I removed my shirt, tucked it through a belt buckle, and walked down Melpomene towards home.

Grace Sheehan fell down a flight of stairs and broke her neck. Roger Palmer had fallen down a flight of stairs and broken his neck. This was too many coincidences involving the same group of people, and the common denominator was Wendell Sheehan. Abby had said it was almost like Roger Palmer's death was a blueprint for Wendell's, but there were more similarities between Roger's death and Grace Sheehan's. Was it possible that Wendell was somehow involved in both accidents?

At Coliseum Square, I looked to see if the car was parked in the same place, and cursed myself for being a paranoid idiot when it wasn't. There was no reason for anyone to be staking out my house. But my job required me to be suspicious. If it *was* something, at least I'd alerted Abby to it.

I climbed my steps and unlocked the front door. When I pushed it open, a large manila envelope skidded across the floor to behind my sofa. I locked the door behind me, picked up the envelope and carried it to my desk. I checked my phone for messages—there weren't any—and sat down and opened the envelope.

It contained about thirty sheets of paper. Each sheet had photocopies of three checks drawn on an account titled WENDELL SHEEHAN, DISCRETIONARY FUNDS, and each check was for five thousand dollars. All of them were made out to Kenneth Musgrave. The name sounded vaguely familiar, but I couldn't place it. The top sheet was dated October 1, 1999. Each successive check was dated the first of the month, and every check was for five thousand dollars. Wendell had paid Kenneth Musgrave over five hundred thousand dollars in a little less than ten years.

Who the hell was he, and what was the money for? Blackmail? And who'd put the envelope through my mail slot?

Curiouser and curiouser, I thought as I turned on my computer.

CHAPTER FIVE

LOREN MCKEITHEN TOSSED THE photocopied checks onto my coffee table.

"I have no idea who Kenneth Musgrave is, or what this is about," he said. "It could be blackmail, but it could also be any number of other things. I don't see what relevance it has to what's going on now, though. You think this might have something to do with Wendell's death?"

He picked up his tall glass of vodka tonic and took a drink. My own drink sat untouched on the table. Loren had finally returned my call while I was at the gym. It had been almost a week since I'd worked out (I find it good for clearing the mind). He always brought a bottle of premium vodka with him when he came to my apartment. He was one of those people whom drink never seemed to affect. I'd learned that it was best to be on my guard around him—and vodka, no matter how premium, was not my friend in that situation.

"There's a reason the name isn't familiar to you," I

said, ignoring his question. "I did some poking around after I got these. Kenneth Musgrave was Grace Sheehan's half-brother. They had different fathers."

"Then it was probably a family thing."

I picked up my glass and took a sip. It was damned good vodka.

"Family members have stooped to blackmail before. Regardless, I'm curious as to who thought I should know about this—and why."

"I'm sure you'll get to the bottom of it," Loren said.

He was a short man, about five-foot-five and always impeccably dressed, but he had a presence that made him seem much taller. He'd always had a bit of a paunch, and in the years since Katrina it had expanded into a full-blown potbelly. He wore round-framed glasses and slicked his dark hair down, claiming it helped hide the balding. (It didn't.) Like a lot of people in New Orleans with racial mixing in their genetic history, his skin was toffee color. He was probably the best criminal lawyer in town, and he was very active in gay politics. We'd been friends of a sort before our run-in during the last case he'd referred to me.

"I appreciate your taking on the case," Loren said. "I wasn't sure you would."

Which is why you had Cordelia pressure Barbara into pressuring me, I thought.

"Which begs the question, why me?" I replied.

He smiled enigmatically. "I prefer to work with the best. What happened last time wasn't personal. I want you to know that."

It wasn't quite an apology, and the compliment was meaningless. He'd throw me under the bus again if he thought it was in his client's best interests. Loren's first allegiance was to his clients. That made him a great lawyer, but also made him slippery to deal with. I'd made the mistake of trusting him once, and I never would again.

"If I'd thought it was personal, I wouldn't have taken the case—and you sure as hell wouldn't be sitting on my couch," I said evenly.

"Fair enough." He opened his briefcase and placed a file folder on the coffee table. "Here's the autopsy report you requested."

I resisted the urge to start reading it.

"Tell me, Loren, what exactly is the point of my investigation?"

"Didn't Cordelia explain what she wanted?"

He kept his voice and face expressionless.

"If you'll excuse my language, it was a bunch of horseshit."

"Well, that's honest, at any rate."

"Which is more than I can say for either Janna or Cordelia."

"Oh?"

"I know you can't tell me anything, but if they gave the police the same stories, I don't understand why Cordelia hasn't been arrested. Scratch that. I *do* understand why she hasn't been arrested."

"You think the police are cutting her slack because of who she is."

"You tell me. A man is shot to death, someone is found holding the murder weapon, her fingerprints are on the gun, her hands test positive for residue, yet she hasn't been arrested. How often does that happen?"

"When you put it that way, it does look suspicious. Maybe it's because she has the best attorney in New Orleans. Maybe it's because she's powerful and has a lot of friends in high places that owe her favors. If it were anyone other than Cordelia Spencer Sheehan, they'd probably be in jail. It's not for me to say if that's right or wrong. I work with what I have. My top priority is always the client. I'd have to say Cordelia's position and standing are assets, and I'll use everything I can to protect her."

"You can't tell me you haven't noticed their stories don't mesh. To believe them you have to accept that Janna and Cordelia are not only stupid, they're *incredibly* stupid."

"Smart people do stupid things sometimes, Chanse. It happens every day, and more often than you think. I seem to remember you handling a murder weapon fairly recently."

"True, but when I handled it, it wasn't a murder weapon."

"Touché."

Loren put down his drink.

"Put yourself in Cordelia's place for a minute, Chanse. She's a mother who walked into her own drawing room and discovered her son's dead body. Obviously, she wasn't thinking clearly."

I took another small sip from the drink and put it down.

"You might be able to convince a jury of that, but I don't buy it, and I don't think you do, either. And we both know Venus and Blaine won't believe it for a second."

"Leave the legal strategy to me, Chanse. That isn't what you were hired to do. Find someone outside the family to pin this on."

Loren polished off his drink. I picked up his empty glass and went into the kitchen to mix him another vodka tonic.

"It seems to me that all Cordelia has to do is blame Janna, and all Janna has to do is blame Cordelia," I said as I carried the drink back in and sat down.

"What's wrong with that equation, Chanse?"

When I didn't answer, Loren went on.

"Cordelia's gotten herself into a bad situation, certainly, and she may truly believe Janna killed Wendell. But the most important thing for Cordelia is to protect the family name. Apparently you didn't grasp that when you met with her."

"She came through loud and clear. I just don't get it."

"You don't *have* to get it, Chanse. Just do what she wants. Wendell Sheehan had enemies. Focus on them."

"Like Kenny Musgrave?" I said frostily.

"Bingo. I doubt that Cordelia herself slipped those photocopies through your mail slot, but she has plenty of employees. This Kenneth Musgrave may be Grace's half-brother, but he isn't a Sheehan. Neither Cordelia nor Janna will be available to you for future questioning."

He held up his hand as I started to protest.

"I know what you're going to say, but you need to look elsewhere. You won't have access to either Mrs. Sheehan, and they aren't going to let you anywhere near the kids. You'll be fired first. The last thing you want to do is get on the wrong side of Cordelia Spencer Sheehan, Chanse. She's a very vindictive woman—especially when it comes to her family. Just do what she wants. Stay away from them. Wendell had plenty of enemies."

"None of whom had access to his wife's gun or could have gotten into and out of the house without anyone knowing. And there's another thing. Wendell's whereabouts are unaccounted for during three-and-a-half hours that night. He left his campaign office at around eight. According to the Sheehans, he didn't get home until eleven-thirty. It's a fifteen-minute drive, tops."

"Find out where he was and who he was with," Loren said. "Check into Kenneth Musgrave. You might be surprised by what turns up."

That sounded like I was being sent on a wild goose chase. This entire thing went against my grain, and I said so.

Loren laughed. "Once a cop, always a cop," he said. "Nobody's asking you to frame anyone, Chanse. Is it so hard for you to conceive that everything that happened that night happened exactly the way they said it did? Can't you for one minute imagine that neither Janna nor Cordelia killed Wendell?"

"I'd find it a lot easier to believe if they weren't lying," I said.

"Open your mind to the possibility."

Loren removed a check from his briefcase and passed it to me. I looked at it and put the check down on the table.

"Fifty thousand dollars is a lot of money," I said. "Is this a bribe?"

"For God's sake, Chanse. No one is asking you to do anything unethical or immoral. What if, in the course of your investigation, you find out someone else *did* kill Wendell Sheehan? Take this check to the bank, cash it, and do what Cordelia wants. Run your investigation predicated on the idea that neither woman committed this crime. Presumption of innocence, remember? You just need to find someone—anyone—who had reason to want Wendell Sheehan dead, and who doesn't have an alibi for the night of the murder. It's a pretty decent payday—and it's not a bad thing to have Cordelia Spencer Sheehan in your debt."

He stood up, closing his briefcase. I went to see him out.

"And what if I find evidence that Cordelia or Janna actually did kill him?"

"That's my problem, not yours," he said as I unlocked the deadbolt and swung the door open. "All I'm asking is for you to keep an open mind. I know you can do that."

"One last question, Loren."

He paused on the porch. "Shoot."

"What did you think of Wendell Sheehan?"

His face became a mask.

"I think Wendell would have been a really good friend to the gay community in Congress—and we need all the friends we can get. Don't quote me on this, but personally I couldn't stand the man."

He walked down my front steps and got into his BMW.

I looked across the park. The car was back.

I shut the door slowly, went to my desk, and picked up my cell phone, then waited for Abby to answer.

"Chanse!" she breathed into my ear. "I was just about to call you. You wouldn't believe—"

I interrupted her. "The car's out there again."

I walked to the front door and peered through the blinds. It was in the exact same place it had been last night. I squinted, trying to get a look inside. I could make out two men in the front seat, but not much more than that. The car appeared to have shaded windows.

"You're sure it's the same car?" Abby asked.

"As sure as I can be from this distance. If it's not, it's pretty similar."

"I'll be there in about fifteen. I'll text you when I'm close."

I took a big drink from my glass and carried Loren's glass to the kitchen sink, then stoppered the big bottle of vodka and put it on the living room shelf where I kept my liquor. I resisted checking on the car again. Instead, I paced.

I hadn't told Loren anything about Kenneth Musgrave other than the family connection to the Sheehans. Shortly after Grace Sheehan died the same way

Barbara's husband had, Musgrave somehow came up with the money to buy a gallery on Julia Street, in the Arts District. I'd been there a few times, most recently a few weeks ago, on White Linen Night. The gallery had some pieces I really liked, but they were a little pricey. I tried to remember if I'd met the gallery owner, but couldn't. Whoever had the bright idea to hold a big art block party in August should be taken out and shot. Everyone was drenched in sweat and packed into the oh-so-welcome air-conditioning in the participating galleries. I have a tendency to be claustrophobic, so I'd tried to examine as much of the art on display as possible before I was forced to flee, screaming.

According to what I'd been able to dig up, Kenneth Musgrave lived in a condo not far from his gallery, and was single. His record was spotty. He'd attended Tulane, but didn't graduate. He never held a job for more than a few months. Since opening the Allegra Gallery, though, he'd made a serious name for himself in the New Orleans art world. He had exclusive agreements with some top local artists, and had curated a show at the Museum of Modern Art in City Park. It was a pretty dramatic change for someone who'd seemed to drift with no direction before.

My phone chirped as I peered through the blinds again. I clicked on the text message button. *Almst thr boss!* Abby's text read.

I slid the phone into my jeans pocket and almost laughed. A gutterpunk girl on a one-speed bicycle that had seen better days was heading downtown on the Coliseum Street side of the park. When she passed under a streetlight, I saw that she had multicolored dreadlocks around her face and wore a pair of ratty overalls cut off at the knees, with a red and white striped T-shirt underneath. Knee-high socks matched the T-shirt. All of the clothing looked like it hadn't been washed in several years. I was certain it was Abby. As she got nearer to the car, she dismounted from her bike and knocked on the passenger side window.

I told myself to relax. *They have no idea who she is or what she's doing, and besides, you don't know if they're dangerous.* Regardless, I left the window and got my gun, tucked it into the back of my jeans, slid the deadbolt open, and stood there, one hand on the doorknob, the other holding apart two slats of the blinds, so I could see what was going on.

Abby was talking to them. Even from the distance I could tell she was playing like she was stoned out of her mind. I cursed myself for asking her to spy for me, and cursed her even more for approaching the car.

Abby waved at the car, climbed back on her bike, and fell over onto the street. The car drove off. Abby got up, dusted herself off, and shook her fist at it.

Once the car was out of sight, I opened my door and went out onto the porch. Abby was walking her bike across the park. She crossed Camp and grinned at me as she hoisted the bike onto her shoulder and climbed my steps.

"Are you insane?" I yelled. "What the hell were you thinking?"

She carried the bike inside and I locked the door behind her, resisting the urge to shake her.

"Just chill for a minute, boss. They had no clue I'd made them."

She crossed her eyes, shut them halfway, and weaved.

"*Dude, I think I'm lost. Do you know where Camp Street is?*"

It was pretty convincing, I had to admit.

"The suckers just thought I was some gutter girl, so stoned I didn't know where the hell I was."

She removed her watch and handed it to me with a wink. It looked like it had cost six dollars at Wal-Mart.

"Why are you giving me this?"

"You *really* need to get into the twenty-first century, Chanse."

She grabbed the watch from my hand and pointed the face at me, pressing the button on the side, clearly delighted with herself.

"There. You can use it as a headshot for your next batch of business cards."

I sat down hard on the couch.

"That's a—"

"Digital camera, yes. You're welcome. I just got it in the mail today—it's so cool. And how cool is it that I got a chance to use it already! Now we can download the pictures on your computer. I got a good one of the passenger, I think, but I wasn't able to get the driver."

She reached into the filthy backpack over her left shoulder and dug out a cord, then sat at the computer, plugged the cord into a port and attached it to her watch.

"Which reminds me, boss. What have you done to warrant being watched by the Feds?"

"The *Feds*?"

"Maybe not Feds specifically, but they reeked of law enforcement. I don't think they were NOPD. We get plenty of them at the Catbox Club and I know 'em when I see 'em. They're usually lousy tippers."

She frowned at the computer screen. Her fingers flew over the keyboard.

"Which is really annoying, since our tax dollars pay their salary. I say cut out the middleman and I'll just tip myself, thank you very much. Ah, there we go."

I looked over her shoulder as the pictures downloaded and she moved them into a folder she created on the desktop. She quickly named the folder "Feds," opened it, highlighted all the pictures, and opened them.

"That thing takes pretty damned good pictures," I said.

"You can get one at surveillance.com," she said as she enlarged the pictures. "They have all kinds of cool stuff on there."

There were shots of the car, and one good shot of the guy in the passenger seat. He looked to be about thirty-five, with dark, brush-cut black hair, a square jaw, thin lips, and strong cheekbones. He wore a dark jacket over a dark tie and a white shirt. His eyes were hidden behind dark glasses. Abby was right. If he wasn't a Federal agent, I'd eat her watch camera.

"Print that one out. Did you get one of the license plate?"

"Of course I did. Do I look like an amateur? It should be the next picture."

She clicked it open and printed it.

"I'll have Jephtha trace the plate when I get home."

"Nice work, Abby."

I removed the pictures from the printer tray and took them to the couch. It was entirely possible that whatever agency these guys worked for, they weren't after *me*. I couldn't think of anything I might have done to warrant being watched. And they weren't *following* me—I would have noticed that. They were just watching my apartment.

But watching for what? And why? It was more than a little unsettling.

Had I done something to warrant Federal involvement? These days, who knew what would pique their interest?

"That's another lunch you owe me," Abby said. She lit a cigarette and plopped into my reclining chair. "And when I tell you about my afternoon, you're not only going to buy me dinner at Commander's, you're going to give me a raise."

"I'll take it under advisement," I responded as usual, placing the pictures on the coffee table.

"You don't want to hear about my little chat with

Carey Sheehan? You could always wait for the report.
I was writing it up when you called."

"Don't tempt me to fire you."

"Pooh."

She blew smoke in a steady stream up into the ceiling
fan.

"All right. After I left Slice this afternoon I went home
and checked on a few things. The Sheehans aren't
Catholic, so where would they send their kids?"

"Newman."

Newman was a private school on Jefferson Avenue
where wealthy Uptown non-Catholics sent their kids.

"Okay, of course they go to Newman, that didn't require a lot of thinking." She flicked ash into the carved-
glass ashtray on the coffee table. "Or, rather, Alais *went*
there, Carey still does. He's on the swim team. I found
out when they practice, and headed over there and
waited. I did the schoolgirl look, as you suggested. And
you were right, Carey is very hormonal. He's going to
be a looker when he grows up."

"Spare me the pedophilic details."

She made a face.

"I waited until he was heading for his bicycle, then
called his name. I pretended I was an old friend of his
sister's, and was wondering how Alais was doing. I'd
lost her cell number, and was only in town for a couple
of days before I left to go back to school, and it would
be great to see her. Luckily, one of the kids yelled at
us before Carey could ask my name. *Hey, Carey, is that
your babysitter?* I remember the type. I hated them

when I was in high school. Poor Carey turned beet red. So, I put my arm around him, kissed him on the cheek, and looked the asshole right in the face. 'I'm his date,' I told him, 'and he's more of a man than you'll ever be.' You should have seen the look that smug little bastard gave me. Of course, Carey was grateful, so I suggested we go for coffee. We went to the CC's at the corner of Jefferson and Magazine.

"That's one lonely kid, Chanse. All the other kids at swim practice were in groups, laughing and joking and horsing around. Carey was by himself. No one talked to him or anything. I felt bad for him. He kind of reminds me of what Jephtha must have been like at that age— kind of geeky, all bones and angles."

"That sounds like Jephtha now," I teased her.

She gave me the finger and went on with her story.

"We sat in a back booth at CC's. He just shrugged when I offered my condolences about his stepfather. I got the sense he wasn't very close to Wendell. I wanted to ask about his real dad, but didn't want to tip my hand, so I asked about Alais again. That's when it got really interesting.

"Alais hasn't left the house since she came back from Ole Miss. She hardly leaves her room. A shrink comes by three times a week to talk to her. Carey doesn't know what it's all about, but his mother and his grandmother are really worried. He thinks she got into some kind of trouble at Ole Miss. How did he say it? She was completely different when she'd come home for spring break. Then she was always in a good mood, always wanting to go somewhere and take him with her. She was in love, always talking about this boy she was dating. Sometimes she'd sneak out late at night to meet him. Their parents had no clue. I used to do that, too."

"Did she ever mention the boy's name?"

"For some reason she was keeping it all a secret. She didn't want the parents to know she was seeing someone. From what you've told me about the family, the boy was probably someone they wouldn't consider suitable for her. Anyway, poor Carey said Alais was his only real friend, and he'd been looking forward to the summer so they could have more fun. But she came home looking really sick—pale, listless. She doesn't talk to anyone, just stays in her room. She doesn't even turn on her cell phone. If any of her friends call the house, she won't talk to them.

"He looked so sad. My heart almost broke for the poor kid. And then he saw what time it was, mumbled something, and tore out of there. I guess his mother keeps him on a tight leash."

Her eyes glinted. I sensed that she hadn't finished.

"And . . . ?" I said.

"Before he left, Cary told me that Alais was a Kappa up at Ole Miss. So, I called the Kappa house and spoke to the housemother. I am so glad I never joined a sorority! If Mrs. Fisk is any indication of what housemothers are like, God help sorority girls. Very judgmental, and into all their business. I pretended I was Janna Sheehan."

"Nicely done, Abby. You never cease to amaze me."

She stuck her tongue out.

"Thank you. It *was* a damned good job. I said I was calling because I knew she'd be concerned about Alais and would want an update on how she was doing. It was a risk, but it's not like I was going to see her in person. I figured a housemother would have a maternal interest in the girls. I also figured that it wouldn't even occur to the Sheehans to let the housemother know how Alais was doing. If I was wrong, I could just hang up. No harm, no foul, right? But I was right. Mrs. Fisk hasn't heard a word from the Sheehans or Alais since the girl came home, and did she ever want to talk. I told her that Alais wasn't getting any better, she was being medicated for depression, and her shrink was at his wit's end because she told him nothing. Did Mrs. Fisk know anything that could help the poor girl out?"

She leaned forward.

"You're going to *love* this, Chanse."

"You've pretty much already earned a dinner at Commander's," I said.

"Great. So, Mrs. Fisk tells me, 'Poor Alais hasn't been the same since her boyfriend died.'"

"Let me guess—he fell down the stairs and broke his neck," I said, half joking.

She looked like she'd swallowed a canary, and it had been quite tasty.

"No, but could you imagine if he had? Once that woman started talking, she wouldn't stop. Most of it was nonsense, but I finally got his name out of her. I found as much as I could about it on the local paper's website."

She reached into her backpack, pulled out a folder and handed it to me. I opened the folder. A handsome young black face stared at me, next to the headline, STUDENT KILLED IN ROBBERY. He was wearing a jacket and tie—it looked like a school photo—and seemed vaguely familiar, but I couldn't place him. His name was Jerrell Perrilloux and he was from New Orleans.

"He was found on a Sunday morning when he didn't show up for work at Starbucks," Abby explained. "His manager kept calling him, and was worried when he got no answer. So after work he went by Jerrell's apartment to check on him. The door was ajar and he found the body. Jerrell's computer and cell phone were missing, but nothing else."

"Poor kid," I said.

I rifled through the printouts. The police had no leads. He'd last been seen on a Saturday afternoon by the girl he was dating, but her name wasn't released to the papers—no doubt the fine hand of the Sheehan family, although it seemed odd that they had strings to pull in upstate Mississippi.

"I can see why Alais is having problems," I said.

"Mrs. Fisk—the racist bitch—made it clear she didn't approve of Alais's taste in boys. And apparently some of Alais's sorority sisters didn't much care for the notion of one of their Kappa sisters dating a black boy. The police questioned all of them, but found nothing.

Alais and Jerrell pretty much kept as low a profile as they could in a little town like Oxford."

"Maybe the romance started before then. Did you—"

"I was just getting started on looking into him when you called," she interrupted. "Jerrell went to Warren Easton, and I don't imagine students at Newman have much call to mix with public school kids—at least not if Cordelia was their grandmother. And Jerrell was a year ahead of Alais at Ole Miss. I'll get back to work on it at home."

She slid the picture of the car's license plate into her bag.

"Anything else? Should I catch up to Carey again? I didn't really ask him about what happened Monday night."

"Give that a rest for now. See what you can find out about Jerrell and his family."

I filled her in on my conversation with Loren. He'd been clear we were to stay away from the Sheehan family, but Jerrell Perrilloux wasn't a Sheehan.

"So keep looking into this kid—it may be nothing, but . . ."

Abby hoisted her backpack over her shoulder.

"It's interesting how people who get close to the Sheehan family keep dying," she finished my thought drily, adding, "I hope that doesn't include you and me."

"That makes two of us," I said.

CHAPTER SIX

TRULY, TIMING IS EVERYTHING. When a bullet whizzes past you unexpectedly, it doesn't happen in slow motion. Time doesn't stand still. One moment, you are peering through your blinds before starting to turn away. In a matter of seconds, you hear the crack of the gun and the window shatters.

I felt the bullet buzz past my ear and heard it crash into a wall somewhere behind me. Instinct was already driving me downward as awareness dawned of what had happened. My hands were over my head, my heart was pounding, and my ears were ringing as shattered glass rained over my body. I hit the floor with a bone-jarring thud.

But I felt nothing. As my mind formed coherent thoughts again, I wondered if another bullet was coming.

I'd stayed up late rehashing what Abby told me. About an hour after she'd left, she'd e-mailed me her report on her conversations with Carey Sheehan and

Mrs. Fisk. I'd read them several times, and drank more of Loren's vodka. There was something there I couldn't find, and sometimes a bit of vodka helps lubricate my thought process. I'd finally given up around one in the morning and gone to bed, figuring that whatever was there might be clearer after a good night's sleep. I didn't set the alarm. My mind was exhausted from processing information, and it wouldn't hurt to allow myself some extra rest. So I'd woken up late this morning.

I'd just put an English muffin in the toaster when I had the bright idea of checking to see if the car was there again. Still in my underwear, I'd opened the door blinds and looked. There was no car, and as I'd turned away, thinking, *You really are getting paranoid*, the window exploded.

I lay on the floor taking deep breaths to slow my heart rate. I was having a major adrenaline rush. My hands and legs were shaking. In that state, I would be an easy target for the shooter—if, in fact, he was still out there waiting for another shot at me. My gun was across the room, locked in my desk drawer. I checked to see if I could make it to the desk without being in view. The door blinds flapped in the breeze. I heard normal morning traffic outside on Camp Street. The front gate hadn't squeaked, so no one had come inside. But the shooter might decide to finish the job. My cell phone was sitting on my desk. I had to get there.

I crawled on my stomach across the Oriental carpet between the couch and the coffee table. If I'd stood there a couple of seconds longer, I'd be dead now. I pushed the panic down as best I could. I had to get my gun. I had to get to my phone. I had to get help.

I managed to reach my desk. I opened the bottom drawer, retrieved the gun, and willed my hands to stop shaking so I could make sure it was loaded. I switched the safety off and sat with my back to the desk. I had a clear view of the front door and a clear shot at anyone who approached it. I flipped open my cell phone and somehow hit speed dial.

"Casanova."

"Venus, it's Chanse." I focused on controlling my breathing, fighting down the hysteria threatening to take over. "Someone just shot out the window in my front door." I took another deep breath. "The bullet missed me by inches."

She immediately went into cop mode. "Are you hurt?"

"No."

"I'll call for backup. We're on our way."

I closed the phone and let it drop to the floor. Both my arms were bleeding where the glass had nicked me. Splinters of glass embedded in my skin twinkled in the morning light. Now that I'd noticed them, they stung. I brushed at the splinters with my gun, stood up and leaned against the desk. I heard sirens, getting closer.

Why would someone shoot at me? Cordelia?

I remembered Loren's warning: *You don't want to get on her bad side.*

"That's crazy," I said aloud. So far, I hadn't really turned up anything the police couldn't have found. There was no reason for Cordelia to have me shot. Sure,

Abby had talked to Carey, but Cordelia didn't know Abby worked for me. Even if Carey said something to her, Abby's cover as a friend of his sister's should have worked, although Alais could have exposed the lie.

I dismissed that. Alais was depressed and on medication. Carey had told Abby she didn't talk to anyone. He may have thought that if he mentioned it to her she would talk to him, but most likely it hadn't gone any further than that. It had to be something—or someone—else.

Who had I pissed off enough to want me dead? You can't be a private eye without making enemies. I ran through recent cases in my mind, but nothing, no one, came to me.

"You're not thinking too clearly."

I laughed when I realized I was talking out loud. I heard footsteps on the stairs.

"Chanse?" Venus called.

"I'm in here, Venus."

I heard a couple of other cars drive up, car doors slamming. Venus gave instructions to other officers outside. I willed myself to walk to the door. Even with the police there, I wouldn't stand in front of it. I just turned the key in the deadbolt, to unlock it.

"Come on in," I said.

I breathed a sigh of relief as Venus and Blaine walked in, guns drawn. They stepped over the broken glass.

"You okay?" Blaine asked, giving me a once-over.

I raised my shaking arms. "Shook up, mostly. Some cuts from the glass. Nothing serious."

Venus wore a gray pantsuit with a red silk blouse. Her face was all sharp angles made even more prominent by her hair cut close to the scalp. She glanced at the wall where the pocket doors between the living room and the kitchen area were stored, and went to a hole in the plaster to the left of the doorway. "Here's the slug," she said. She looked at me critically. "Go put some clothes on," she directed.

I went to the bedroom and threw on a pair of black sweatpants, an LSU National Champions T-shirt, and my house shoes. I brushed glass splinters off my arms in the bathroom, wincing a bit, and started the hot water running. Thin trails of blood webbed my forearms. I splashed water on my face and took a few deep breaths before washing off the blood. I put bandages on some of the bigger cuts and returned to the living room.

"From the trajectory of the bullet, whoever shot at you was shooting down," Venus said as I stood next to her. She looked out the broken window. Someone had pulled up the blinds. Across the park, uniformed officers knocked on doors. A couple of other uniforms searched underneath one of the big live oaks where the mystery car had been parked. Venus turned to me.

"Who the hell did you piss off?"

"Your guess is as good as mine," I said.

"You on a job?" Blaine asked.

"You know I can't talk about my cases," I replied.

"You will this time, bud. When people are taking pot-shots at you, I don't want to hear that confidentiality bullshit. Start talking."

I walked back into the kitchen and poured myself more coffee, resisting the urge to add whiskey. I poured cups for Venus and Blaine and handed them over the bar.

"Tuesday morning, Cordelia Spencer Sheehan hired me to look into her son's death."

Venus and Blaine exchanged glances I couldn't read. In a low, neutral voice, Venus said, "You think maybe this has something to do with the case?"

I gulped down coffee. "Right now I don't know what to think. But for the last two nights, I noticed a car parked out by that tree." I pointed to where the officers were examining the ground. "Last night, I got Abby to spy on the guys in the car. She took photos of the license plate and the guy in the passenger seat. They're on my computer."

"You'll need to print those up for us," Venus said. "Blaine, you mind waiting outside for the lab guys?"

He opened his mouth to say something, but she shook her head slightly.

"You know we're on the Sheehan murder," Venus said when we were alone. She sat on the couch. I plopped down in the reclining chair. "Tell me what you've found."

"Nothing, really."

One of the most difficult parts of being a private eye is dealing with the police, especially when you're working the same case. I personally wasn't comfortable not coming clean with the cops if my client had broken the law. This wasn't the first time one of Venus's and my cases overlapped, but we'd come to an understanding in the past. Although she didn't like me working her cases, a few times we'd shared information unofficially that eventually led to an arrest. As a private eye, I could cut some corners she couldn't.

"I interviewed both Mrs. Sheehans and found some interesting discrepancies in their stories," I said.

"Imagine that. Go on."

"I suppose it doesn't mean anything, certainly not enough to have me killed. Witnesses' stories are often contradictory."

"This the only case you're on now?"

I nodded. "Abby's looking into an insurance fraud case, but that's pretty cut-and-dried. Let me ask you a question."

"Just tell me what happened this morning."

I exhaled. "I woke up. I made coffee, did my usual morning routine, and came into the living room to work at my computer. I decided to check to see if the car was outside. I went to the window in the door and looked through the blinds. The car wasn't there, and as I turned away the window exploded."

"Did you notice anything out of the ordinary?"

I closed my eyes and thought for a moment. "Sorry. All I was looking for was the car."

"You didn't see anyone in the park?"

I thought again. "There may have been people at the other end, but this end of the park was empty."

"How could the shooter have known you'd come to the window?"

"He couldn't have. It wasn't part of my routine. Come to think of it, I hardly ever look out that window."

She kept watching my face. I could feel it color. I'd been a cop, so it wasn't hard to figure out what she was thinking. Someone wanted to shoot me, and they just watched my apartment, waiting for me to move into the window? Wouldn't it have been easier to wait for me to leave and follow me until they got a better shot? Why take this kind of a chance? Unless whoever it was *wanted* me to know I was being hunted.

"If I hadn't turned away from the window I would have been shot," I said, trying to keep my voice even. "I felt the bullet whiz by my head."

"Obviously someone shot at you, Chanse," she said calmly. "I'm just wondering why. And why they took such a risk."

"And obviously, I don't know the answer to that."

I heard my voice rise, and took another deep breath.

"This car just showed up two nights ago?"

"I only noticed it two nights ago. I was out of town until Tuesday afternoon."

Her face softened. "That's right. I'm sorry, Chanse. How's your mother?"

"She's responding to the treatments. The doctors are cautiously optimistic."

"Good."

Blaine led a couple of men through the front door. "Here are the lab techs," he said.

Venus stood up. "Chanse, print those pictures and we'll continue this in your bedroom."

I did as she ordered. Blaine and Venus followed me into the bedroom. Venus glanced at the pictures, then put them in her shoulder bag.

"I'll trace the plates and see what we can find."

She filled Blaine in on what I'd already told her.

"The bullet had to have been fired from a higher level," he said. "But there are no shell casings or anything around the tree, and no signs that anyone had been in it. Is there anything you aren't telling us, Chanse?"

"No," I said, fighting the urge to scream at them. They were just doing their jobs, after all.

"What can you tell me about the house on the corner of Terpsichore and Coliseum?" Blaine asked.

"You probably know more about it than I do," I snapped.

Blaine's partner was a mover and shaker in the Coliseum Square Association.

"The house is empty," Blaine told Venus. "My best guess: if the shooter wasn't in the tree, he had to be on the second floor of that house." He turned back to me. "The house has been empty since after Katrina, and no, I don't know anything about it."

I closed my eyes. An empty house on the other side of the park. There was no telling how long the shooter had been there, waiting for a chance at me. I thought of the last two nights. How many times had I been out there on the porch? When I'd watched Paige walk to her car. When I'd walked Loren to his BMW. When I'd walked with Abby. The shooter had a much better shot all three of those times than he'd had this morning. Why not shoot me then?

Because there had been other people around all three times, potential witnesses. He wanted me when I was alone.

I started to shake again. I mentioned my theory to Blaine and Venus.

"And those three times, was the mystery car there?" Venus asked. She was scribbling in her notepad and didn't look up.

"Paige and Loren, yes. Not for Abby. After Abby pulled her little stunt, the car took off, so it wasn't there when I let her out."

I closed my eyes, remembering. Abby had hoisted her bike over her shoulder and carried it out the front door. I'd stood and watched as she carried it down the steps, and stayed there with the porch light shining directly on me, until she went through the gate and pedaled away down Camp Street.

I might as well have painted a bull's-eye on my chest.

"I'm going to call for a search warrant," Blaine said, and returned to the living room.

"Are you sure you can't think of anyone who'd want you out of the way?" Venus asked gently.

"I swear I can't."

"Okay." She looked out the bedroom door. "Looks like the techs are wrapping up. We'll get a warrant and search that empty house. I'll call you if we find anything."

"Thanks."

After they had cleared out, I poured myself another cup of coffee. I had to do something about the window. I called Gus, the handyman for Barbara's properties. He told me he'd contact a glazier. I started sweeping up the broken glass. I'd pretty much finished when my cell phone rang.

"MacLeod."

"Chanse, dear, this is Barbara." Her voice was shaky. "Gus just called. He's on his way to your apartment to board up the window and wait for the glazier. Are you all right?"

"A little shook up, a few cuts here and there from broken glass, but other than that, I'm okay."

"Thank God. As soon as Gus gets there, would you mind coming over here? We need to have a chat."

That sounded ominous.

"I'll be there as soon as I can."

I changed into jeans and a Polo shirt, and washed my face again. When Gus arrived, I drove over to the Palmer House. Barbara was sitting in the drawing room in a wingback chair, in jeans and a T-shirt, with a mimosa in her hand. She wasn't wearing makeup. Her eyes were worried as she walked over and examined the bandages on my arms.

"Are you sure you're all right, dear?"

I nodded.

"Would you like a drink?"

I shook my head.

"Thank God you're all right, dear. You don't think . . ." Her voice trailed off.

"I don't know what to think." I gave her what I hoped was a reassuring smile. "You wanted to talk to me?"

She bit her lip.

"Would you mind explaining to me why exactly your assistant was talking to Archie Larousse yesterday morning?"

For a moment I couldn't answer her, it came so far from left field. "How—" I finally spluttered.

"Cordelia is paying you to find someone outside her family to hang Wendell's murder on. I knew that was what she wanted. But why dig up this past dirt, Chanse?"

She drained her glass. Her hands shook as she lit a cigarette. I'd never seen her smoke before. She saw me watching her and snapped, "I smoke from time to time, not that it's any of your business. Usually when I'm under stress. Wendell wasn't my favorite person, but I can assure you I didn't kill him."

"I never thought you did, Barbara."

"Thank you for that."

She poured another glass and handed it to me.

"Champagne will calm your nerves, dear."

Her ash fell onto the white carpet. She ignored it and sat back down.

"I'm sorry you were shot at, Chanse, that I got you involved in this. But what was that girl doing talking to Archie Larousse?"

"When I was here the other morning, you made it very clear that you don't like Cordelia Sheehan. But you interceded with me to take her on as a client. You said you owed her. And you were clearly unhappy about it. I thought if I could find out what she was holding over you, I could help free you from her."

"By digging into my past?"

I nodded. She twirled a strand of hair around her right index finger.

"There's nothing you can do, Chanse. I'm trapped. I've been trapped for almost thirty years. But I do appreciate what you're trying to do for me."

"Roger didn't fall down the stairs, did he?"

I braced myself for an explosion. Instead, her posture loosened and she looked sad. She drained her glass and poured another mimosa.

"I haven't talked about this to anyone, Chanse. Maybe it would help if I did now. I was so young and stupid. Archie Larousse is a liar. He always has been. He told Abby that I killed Roger, and that the Sheehans pressured the police into ruling it an accident and closing down the investigation, right?"

"Is it true, Barbara?" I said softly. "You can tell me."

"Just like Cordelia threatened, all those years ago. That miserable bitch." She wiped her eyes. "I didn't kill Roger. I was young and stupid. I married out of my element. I didn't belong in the Garden District, and everyone made sure I knew it. They were polite when Roger was around—he was a Palmer, after all—but whenever he wasn't around they were politely insulting and condescending. Roger was very kind to me. And how did I repay him? By proving all those bitches right and having a cheap affair."

"With Wendell Sheehan."

She nodded.

"He was very handsome, and he was young. I never should have married Roger. I was fond of him, but I didn't love him. It was the money—and this house. I grew up really poor, Chanse, and I always thought money would make everything better. When I met Roger and he wanted to marry me, I thought what the hell. I don't know what I was thinking. I was bored, I guess. Roger was always busy with his clubs and his friends and managing his money. I didn't have any friends. And Wendell . . . I first met him at the Rex Ball. He was fresh out of law school, his father was the governor, and he didn't care that I was from the West Bank. He flirted with me, made me feel like I was special. Even after I told him I wasn't interested, he kept after me. Finally, one day I said to myself, *Why not? No one ever has to know.*

"Stupid, stupid girl. He kept a suite at the Roosevelt Hotel. I used to meet him there on Wednesday afternoons. It was, I don't know, exciting. Roger had no idea."

"What really happened the night Roger died?"

She smiled bitterly. "Undoubtedly you've discovered that my alibi was worthless? That was Cordelia's idea. I was *supposed* to be at that fundraiser. But that was the day I found out I was pregnant. I thought Roger would be happy. He came into my room to see what I was wearing. Roger always helped me dress—I didn't know what the hell I was doing. I told him my news. He just stared at me. I remember thinking he wasn't taking it as I'd thought he would. And then he said, *You can take the girl out of the West Bank, but apparently you can't take the West Bank out of the girl.*

"I asked him what he was talking about, and he started screaming at me, demanding to know who the father was. I was shocked. I had no idea what he meant. Apparently he'd had the mumps in his early twenties. I can see by your face you don't know what that means. The mumps are a perfectly safe illness for a child—no lasting effects. But they can leave an adult male sterile."

"It was Wendell's child."

She nodded.

What a nightmare that must have been.

"I'd never seen Roger so angry. He stormed out of my room. I didn't know what to do. I didn't even know he had a temper he could lose. I could hear him screaming and breaking things. And then I did a really stupid thing. I called Wendell. He rushed to my rescue like some kind of chevalier. If only I'd known. I should have packed my things and left, let Roger divorce me. But I wasn't thinking clearly."

"Wendell killed Roger," I said.

"He told me to lock myself in my room until he arrived. He said he'd talk to Roger, clear things up. I heard them yelling at each other—and fighting. Then Roger screamed. There was a crash, and silence. I came out of my room. Wendell was standing at the top of the stairs. Roger was at the bottom, dead.

"I panicked. Wendell was like in a trance, shock I guess. But when I went to call the police, he stopped me. He told me it had been an accident, but if we called the police, everything would come out—the affair, the baby. So he called Cordelia, and she told us what to do.

"We left the house, left Roger lying there. I went to the fundraiser, but I was so upset, I couldn't go inside. I couldn't let anyone see me. I thought people would look at me and know what had happened. Cordelia was furious with me later. *You were supposed to be seen, you little fool. After all the trouble I've gone to in order to save your worthless West Bank hide, you couldn't follow instructions? I should just let you go to jail, you stupid girl.*"

Her mimicry of Cordelia was ruthless. Tears were running down her face, but she went on without a sob or a break.

"Archie Larousse was on the Sheehan payroll. He was crooked, but I never knew the extent of it. I know he doctored the evidence, and Cordelia pulled strings from the governor's mansion to get the whole thing hushed up."

"But if Wendell killed Roger, what hold did Cordelia have on you?"

"My daughter," she whispered. "Cordelia threatened that if I ever told anyone the truth about that night, she'd take my daughter away. Larousse doctored the evidence, all right. Cordelia once showed me the file. His report made it look as though I had killed Roger.

The payments she made to him? Somehow they finagled it so it appeared like *I* had paid him. And of course, Wendell's alibi was perfect. *She* alibied him. Who would doubt the First Lady of Louisiana? She told me if I ever talked, Larousse would leave the country and she'd see to it that I spent the rest of my life behind bars."

She wiped her cheeks, her hands still shaking.

"Of course, as Brenda got older, I never told her who her real father was. How could I? Cordelia used that against me, too." Her voice hardened. "*How would Brenda like it if she found out her mother was a whore and a murderess? It's not too late to prove her true paternity. Do you want to do that to your daughter?*"

My head was spinning. "My God," was all I could say.

"How do you think I found out about Abby talking to Larousse, Chanse? He called Cordelia for instructions after Abby contacted him. Cordelia told him what to do, what to say. And then she called me, to twist the knife and renew her threats. She'll stoop to anything, Chanse, to protect her family. Trust me, if I was going to kill a Sheehan, it wouldn't have been Wendell. I would have killed that horrible old witch. I've been tempted to so many times. But what good would that have done anyone?"

"And all this time, you and Wendell . . . ?"

"We never saw each other again, if I could help it. He stayed away from me, and stayed away from Brenda. I couldn't be involved with him after that. I've spent the rest of my life terrified. Terrified that Brenda might find out, terrified that *anyone* would find out. When Charles was alive, she used it to get me to donate to her stupid foundation. *I'd hate for the handsome young husband of yours to find out what you're really like, Barbara. That would be a real tragedy, wouldn't it?*"

She buried her face in her hands.

"Now that you know the truth, do you think I'm horrible, Chanse?" she asked in a small, sad voice.

"No, Barbara, I don't. I'm so sorry. If I'd known, I never would have allowed Abby to—"

The Sheehans had done an excellent job of painting her into a corner—and then held it over her head for thirty years.

"How could you have known, dear? You were trying to help me. You have no idea how much I appreciate that. What are you going to do, now that you know?"

"What can I do? I'm not going to tell anyone."

"I'll deny it all if you repeat it. The irony is that Cordelia told me if I helped her this one last time, if I got you to take the case, she'd destroy the doctored evidence. I'd finally be free of her."

"I'm not going to let Cordelia railroad you, Barbara."

I knelt beside her. She took my hand and gave it a pat.

"Thank you for believing me, dear. You've always been good to me."

My cell phone rang. I ignored it. I felt I should say something to Barbara, but I couldn't think what.

"Aren't you going to answer that?" she asked. "Go ahead, we're done here."

She got up to leave the room. When she reached the door, she turned and gave me a shaky smile.

"Thank you again, dear."

I stared after her as I opened my phone.

"MacLeod."

"This is Janna Sheehan. I need you to come to the house as soon as you can." Her voice was trembling.

"What's wrong?"

"It's my daughter, Alais. She's not in her room or anywhere on the grounds. I think she may have run away."

"I'm on my way."

I felt incredibly tired, probably the aftereffects of this morning's events. As I walked out the front gates of the Palmer House, I had the feeling I was being watched. I looked up and down the street. There was no one in sight. I looked at the house.

Barbara was at one of the upper windows, watching me. She was crying. I raised my hand and waved.

She put her hand against the glass for a moment, then retreated into the shadows. All I could see was the curtains moving as they settled back into place.

CHAPTER SEVEN

JANNA SHEEHAN HERSELF GREETED me and led me to
the library, a big room painted dark coral with white
trim, across the hall from the drawing room, whose
door was shut. The library walls were covered with
built-in shelves packed with books. Janna looked like
she'd been crying and hadn't slept. Her eyes were shot
through with red. Her hair was slightly disheveled, and
her face was without makeup. She wore jeans and a
shapeless blouse. Her feet were bare, and her fingernails looked chewed. A vein pulsed in her throat; her
hands clenched and unclenched spasmodically. The
slightly sad but together woman I'd met a few days
earlier was gone—or at least, the iron control she'd
exercised over herself had unraveled.

"You've got to find her," she said, her lips a taut line
in her face. Her voice had a note of rising hysteria.

"We'll find her," I said in my calmest voice, pulling
my pad from my shoulder bag. "Start at the beginning.
When did you last see Alais?"

She swallowed, closed her eyes, and thought for a moment.

"Before I went to bed I checked in on her. She seemed fine. Well, no. She hasn't been *fine* since she came home from school. But she didn't seem any different last night, at least nothing out of the ordinary, nothing that I noticed. Maybe I should have paid closer attention. But all she does is stay in her room, on that damned computer. Sometimes she comes down for lunch or dinner, but she never goes outside. She used to love the pool. Last summer I couldn't keep her inside."

She ran her fingers through her hair.

"And this morning?" I said.

"She doesn't come down for breakfast anymore. We used to have breakfast together all the time—Carey, Alais, and myself. Wendell always left the house early. But since she came home in June, Alais never wanted to eat breakfast, so I got out of the habit of waking her up in the morning. I let her sleep in. It drove Wendell crazy. He thought I was coddling her. But she was so depressed."

She cleared her throat.

"I came down to breakfast with Carey. I was going to look in on Alais afterward, but I didn't. I had to run out to an appointment with my doctor. When I got back, Cordelia was calling, and I had to take her damned call before I could to check on Alais."

"Cordelia isn't here?"

I'd have thought the cops would have told her not

to leave town, but then again, the rules didn't seem to apply to the Sheehans.

"She had one of her fundraisers in Baton Rouge last night. We have a house up there. Cordelia called me about the storm. She'd been talking to some of her friends and thought it might be a good idea for us to go there, if need be. She wasn't sure if she should come back to New Orleans."

"Ginevra? It's coming here?"

Janna stared at me as though I were insane.

"Have you not been following it? We're almost directly in the center of the projected path. The governor declared a state of emergency on Wednesday. They're going to call for mandatory evacuation as early as Saturday."

Just as Paige had predicted. I hadn't wanted to think about it. It was too soon. I pushed down the rising panic. We had to find Alais, and fast.

"So, please continue," I said.

"After I spoke to Cordelia I went upstairs to tell the kids about it. Alais wasn't in her room. Her bed hadn't been slept in. There was no note, nothing. I called Cordelia back. She told me to call you."

Interesting that she didn't tell you to call the police and report Alais missing.

"Is anything missing from her room? Clothes, tooth-brush, the kind of things she'd take with her?"

"Her toothbrush is gone. So are her laptop and cell phone. She has a lot of clothes. I can't tell if any of it is missing."

"Did she take a suitcase?"

"I didn't think to check."

I wrote that off to natural panic. "You've tried her cell?"

"She isn't answering it. Or she just isn't taking my calls."

"Does she have a car?"

"She didn't take it. It's still here."

Either someone picked her up or she'd called a cab.

"Then most likely she's in the city. Credit cards?"

She looked at me like I was crazy.

"She has a wallet full of them. American Express, department stores, Visa, several MasterCards. Wendell and Cordelia got them for her. I didn't think she needed more than one. Not that anyone cared for my opinion."

"Do you have a list of them?"

Credit card companies wouldn't give the information to me, but Jephtha might be able to get it online.

"Wendell had a list of all our cards in his computer. I'll print it out for you."

"You need to call the police."

"I can't do that." She looked away. "Cordelia said not to."

I knew it was pointless, but I had to at least try to talk her into it.

"The police have resources I don't have. They can get her cell phone service to pinpoint her location, pull her credit card records and track her down in a matter of hours."

"Cordelia made it clear that the police are not to be contacted."

"Why is that? If finding Alais is the most important thing—"

She met my gaze, lifting her chin defiantly.

"Cordelia doesn't want them involved. That's all you need to know."

Just as I suspected—you'll work with Cordelia when you need to.

"All right," I said. "Tell me, what exactly was going on with Alais? You said she was depressed. Why?"

"Her boyfriend was murdered. Before she went away to school, we were close. I was more like an older sister than a stepmother. After the murder she changed."

"It's no wonder she was depressed."

"The police said it was a robbery gone wrong, but it was a hate crime. What else can you expect from Mississippi cops?"

"Are you saying her boyfriend was black?" I kept my voice neutral, feigning ignorance.

She bristled. "Do you have a problem with that? I don't tolerate racism, Mr. MacLeod."

"It just surprised me." I gave her a reassuring smile. "Wendell and Cordelia didn't have a problem with it?"

"Don't be absurd. Wendell's father fought for civil rights in this state, and Cordelia was right there by his side. That's public record."

I decided not to point out how frequently public positions contradicted private beliefs when it came to race, especially in the South.

"I tried to get Alais to talk to me, but she wouldn't. We hired a therapist to treat her. He came here three times a week. And of course, he wouldn't tell us a goddamn thing. His answer for everything was writing prescriptions. I don't think it's good for a girl her age to be taking so many pills. But no one listened to me."

Once again, she was playing the Sheehan martyr. She was good at it, but it wasn't going to help me find Alais.

"Did she take her prescriptions with her?"

"I didn't think to check her medicine cabinet."

I was tired of games. It was time to play hardball.

"She's been depressed all summer, she had a lot of medication handy, she turns up missing and it didn't occur to you she might try to kill herself?"

Her face drained of color. "Oh, God, no. I don't believe that. Alais would never . . . no."

"You searched the house and the grounds, right?"

"Of course we searched!" she snapped, her eyes flashing. "Carey and Vernita helped."

"Vernita?"

"The housekeeper."

"I'll need to speak to her. Where is she, by the way?"

"I sent her home. It wouldn't have been right to make her stay here. The hurricane? She has her own family, and she needed to get her house ready."

That was why Janna had answered the door herself.

"I'll need her address."

Janna nodded.

"You searched the grounds thoroughly? The pool house? The carriage house?"

"There was no sign of her anywhere. I wouldn't have called you if we'd found her."

"You said she isn't answering her cell phone?"

"I've called it every half hour. It goes straight to voice mail. I leave messages."

"But she took it with her?"

"I didn't see it in her room."

"I'll need to search it."

"Follow me."

Janna swept out of the library. At the bottom of the hanging staircase, she glanced at the closed door to the drawing room and turned to me as if to say something, then started up the stairs, holding on to the railing.

"Is this the staircase where Grace fell?" I asked.

"Yes it is," she said tonelessly, not breaking stride. "She tripped."

Just like Roger Palmer.

We reached the top.

"And that's your room, right?" I indicated a closed door to the immediate right.

"Yes."

"How did Cordelia manage to get downstairs before you did the night your husband died?"

She stopped and looked at me, obviously confused.

"I have no idea. I never thought about it. All I know is she was in the drawing room when I got there." She looked at her door, then at the hallway. If this was an act, she was good. "But that doesn't make sense."

She proceeded along the hallway.

"The police never brought that up? Or Loren Mc-Keithen?"

"Not to me."

I followed her past several closed doors to an open one.

"This is Alais's room. I'll be down in the library if you need anything more."

"About the night your husband was killed—"

She took another few steps before looking back at me, her face expressionless.

"I have nothing else to say to you about that night, Mr. MacLeod. I'll tell you anything you want to know about Alais, but as far as that night is concerned, I've already told you everything."

Does anyone in the house ever tell the truth? I wondered as I watched her walk away.

I don't have a lot of experience with teenagers, so I couldn't say whether Alais's room was typical. It was painted pale blue, and everything in the room matched—the pillows, the comforter on the sleigh bed, the rugs. The big wrought iron bed was centered against the wall to my right, with a nightstand on either side. The table to the left had an iPod docking station on it, but the iPod itself was gone. The table to the right had a phone and a couple of romance novels with covers of bare-chested men clutching large-breasted women with long flowing hair and peasant blouses exposing their shoulders. The spines of both books were intact. I flipped through the pages. Nothing. I put them

down. An open door led to a walk-in closet. I poked
my head inside. Janna was right—there was no way
to tell what Alais might have taken. The clothes were
crammed together on three rods running parallel to
each wall, and there wasn't room for another hanger
anywhere. Each rod had a shelf above it, running the
full length of the wall. Boxes of shoes were neatly
stacked along the right-hand shelf, with a description
of each box's contents neatly lettered in black on the
front: *red open-toe pumps, black stiletto closed-toe,* etc.
The shelf on the left held a complete set of Nancy Drew
hardcovers, their shiny yellow spines facing out. They,
too, looked like they'd never been read. Alongside the
Nancy Drews were enough exercise shoes to stock a
Foot Locker display. None of them looked worn. Some
of them weren't completely laced up.

The shelf along the back wall was covered in hat-
boxes, all neatly lettered with the same black Sharpie.
Alais was very organized. *Do girls still wear hats?* I wondered. I tried to remember the last time I'd seen a teenager in a hat other than a baseball cap, and couldn't. I
pulled down a box and removed the lid. The hat inside
was wide-brimmed and yellow, with the price tag still
on it. I replaced the box and took down another. This
hat was red, with a veil in the front, and also had the
price tag. Alais's bureau probably had a drawer filled
with brand-new, unworn gloves.

If Alais hadn't left the house all summer, where did
all this new stuff come from? I suspected Cordelia had
bought it for her granddaughter.

Nothing in the bedroom seemed out of place. My sister Daphne had kept her room neat when we were growing up, but not like this. Of course, we hadn't had a housekeeper. Daphne had covered her walls with posters of her heartthrobs—the New Kids on the Block, Johnny Depp, Tom Cruise. Cordelia probably didn't allow posters of heartthrobs. Alais's walls were pristine. No framed photographs, no posters, no artwork of any kind. The room had nothing personal in it. No stuffed animals, no trophies, no magazines or books that had actually been read. It was like a movie set. Maybe her room at the sorority house was different.

This room would depress anyone. No wonder she ran away. But there had to be other reasons.

I checked the bathroom. It, too, was pristine. The gold fixtures gleamed. The porcelain tub glistened. Everything on the counter was lined up and organized. There was no toothbrush, and no hairbrush, either. Apparently she had left behind all of her makeup, but, like the clothes, there was so much that it was hard to be sure. I opened the drawers and found more—mascara, eyeliner, lipstick, nail polish, nail files, polish remover—all unopened, in the original packaging. Every shelf in the linen closet was packed with towels, washcloths, and rolls of toilet paper. I opened the medicine cabinet, pulled out my notebook and wrote down the medications, wondering what Alais's therapist had been thinking. Every conceivable antidepressant, anti-anxiety medication, and mood stabilizer I'd ever heard of was there—and some I'd never heard of before—

enough pills for ten people to commit suicide with. The same psychiatrist was listed on every label: DR. ROBERT ENGLESE. I made a note of his name and phone number. He wouldn't tell me anything, but talking to him might turn up something useful. Someone should report him to the AMA. Again there were no empty spaces, so it was safe to assume Alais had not taken any pill bottles with her. Unfortunately, there was no way of knowing how many pills were missing from the bottles.

I returned to the bedroom and went through her bureau. I'd been right. The top drawer was filled with pairs of gloves that still had their price tags attached. There were separate drawers for underwear, socks, shorts, and T-shirts, and everything was sorted by color.

I rifled through the drawers of her desk. Everything was meticulously organized, with nothing out of the ordinary and nothing that would be helpful, not even an address book.

A diary would have been too much to hope for.

I sat down and turned on her Apple computer. The screen asked for a password.

"Her password is *princess*," a voice behind me said softly.

I spun around in the chair.

Carey Sheehan stood leaning against the doorframe, his slender arms crossed. He was wearing an LSU baseball cap, a sleeveless LSU T-shirt, and a ratty pair of jeans shorts about three sizes too big for him. His feet were bare.

"Thanks," I said. "You an LSU fan?"

He came into the room and plopped onto the bed. "Yup."

"I played ball for LSU." I typed in the password. The computer's desktop appeared. "I lettered three years."

"Cool. When did you play?"

I told him. His face lit up with a smile.

"Two SEC championships and two Sugar Bowl wins," he said.

"That's right. You want to go to LSU? It's a great school."

He shrugged. His face went blank again.

"If I go to college. I haven't decided yet."

Like you'll have a choice in this house, I thought.

"So, where do you think your sister went?"

"If she's smart, she got as far away from here as she could."

"Why would you say that?"

"Because that's what I'm going to do as soon as I'm old enough."

I opened her Internet browser, studied her bookmarks and clicked on myspace. Alais's profile page popped up. It wasn't a professional photograph, but it was a good one. She was sitting in the gazebo and laughing, her long, thick red hair hanging past her shoulders on either side of her face.

"You're not happy here?" I asked Carey.

"It's okay, I guess. Things could be worse."

"I'd imagine your father's death was hard on you. I'm sorry about that. Are you doing okay?"

His lower lip quivered. "I'm fine."

I didn't want to make him cry, so I turned back to the computer screen.

"Your sister is quite pretty."

"I took that picture last summer, before she went off to Ole Miss."

"It's a good picture."

I clicked on her friends page and scrolled through them. Alais had over three hundred friends, an almost equal assortment of boys and girls. I wrote the URL address in my notebook, then texted it to Abby with a request that she run down all of the friends.

"You know any of these people, Carey?"

He got up and leaned over my shoulder.

"Some of them are her friends from high school."

"You think she might be with one of them? Who were her closest friends?"

He pointed to a picture of a pretty girl with dark hair.

"Dana Rivers was her best friend at Newman, but she's in Europe. Vienna, I think. As for the rest— I don't know. Alais didn't see anyone this summer. She never left the house. She hardly left this room."

"Did she say anything to you?"

"No. She wouldn't talk to anyone."

I turned around. "No offense, but I don't believe you."

His face turned red. "I don't care what you think."

"Weren't the two of you close?"

"We used to be." His lower lip jutted out. "But she blamed me, and wouldn't talk to me anymore."

"Blamed you for what?"

"Them finding out about Jerrell. But it wasn't my fault."

"Jerrell?"

"Her boyfriend." His lower lip trembled. "It wasn't my fault. I didn't know Mom would go through my computer!"

"What exactly did your mother find?"

"I went up there to visit Alais. I brought my camera. Her and Jerrell and I did a lot of stuff. I took pictures of them together and I downloaded them onto my computer. How was I supposed to know Mom would go snooping? She was *pissed* when she found the pictures. She made me tell her everything. I didn't want to!"

"When was this?"

"Back in May."

Jerrell was murdered in June. "Did your mother tell your father?"

"He wasn't my father!"

"You two weren't close?"

"He wasn't my father," Carey insisted. "My father lives in Hammond."

"What happened the night your stepfather was killed?"

"I don't know. I was in my room."

"You didn't hear anything?"

"I had my headphones on."

"You didn't see him that night?"

"I had dinner with my mom and then I came up-stairs. I was at my computer with my headphones on. I didn't know anything happened until Mom came and told me he was dead."

"You don't seem too upset."

"He didn't care about me. He never came to my swim meets. He never had anything to do with me unless there were other people around. Then it was all 'my son this' and 'my son that.' It was just an act. He didn't care. He was the same with Alais. We used to talk about it. She didn't like him either. And he wasn't nice to my mother. He made fun of her all the time. He yelled at her. He used to make her cry. It made me mad."

"Did he hit her?"

"Not that I know about."

"Do you know if your mother told him about Alais and Jerrell?"

He gave me a sly look. "She must have. Jerrell's dead, isn't he? Alais thought it was my fault, but it wasn't!"

"Alais thought her father killed Jerrell?"

Carey backed toward the door. "I don't know what she thought."

"Did she have a laptop?"

"Yes."

He bolted through the door and was gone.

But he'd given me an interesting piece of informa-tion. I leaned back in the chair, turned to the computer and scrolled to the top of Alais's myspace page. She had kept an online diary. Maybe I was about to get lucky.

I clicked on the link. A window opened, asking for a user name and password. I looked at the address for the myspace page, and typed *Miss Alais* in for the user name and *princess* for the password. A little multicolor wheel spun on the screen. The page came up, with a list of dates serving as links to individual pages.

Bingo.

The most recent entry was dated yesterday. I clicked on it and read.

15 August

The governor called a state of emergency yesterday. I don't know if we're going to evacuate but I don't care. I don't care about anything anymore. Sometimes I hope it does come here and just blows this house off the face of the map. This horrible house. My grandmother's family has done some terrible things. It wouldn't surprise me if all those bad things wound up putting a curse on this place. It's the only thing that makes sense. The sins of the fathers. There were a lot of sins committed in this house.

I wish my mother were still alive. I wish Jerrell were still alive.

I don't know why I bother.

Dr. Englese says I need to let go. But if I do that, Jerrell is gone forever. He says life is for the living, but grieving is normal and we have to do it and get free of it before we can move on.

I wish I'd been the one instead of Jerrell. It was my fault. That's what Dr. Englese doesn't understand.

But I can't tell him. I can't tell anyone the truth.
I need to get away.
But I don't have anywhere to go.

I felt bad for Alais. I, too, had lost someone I loved.

But the entry wasn't very helpful. It told me nothing, really, other than establishing her state of mind. I clicked on the link for 14 August. The page was empty. I clicked back through the earlier entries. All of them were gone. It was possible she had deleted them, but why would she have done that?

I texted Jeph Alais's user name and password, and asked him to see what he could find out about the lost entries, then looked inside the medicine cabinet again.

I had more than a passing acquaintance with many of the medications in there. I'd used them after my boyfriend Paul died, a year before Katrina. They could take the pain away for a short while, but they always wore off and the pain came back. You'd take another pill, holding your breath until the chemicals made their way through your bloodstream to your brain and you forgot. Or you remembered and the chemicals made you not care so much. You just drifted through life, disconnected from everything, not feeling or caring about anything.

Alais was only nineteen.

I turned off the computer and went downstairs to the library. Janna was sitting in the same chair she'd been in before, staring into space, with an open book in her lap. I cleared my throat.

She looked at me, startled.

"What was the problem with Alais dating Jerrell Perrilloux?" I asked.

"I had no problem with it," she said flatly.

"But your husband did."

"Wendell would have had a problem with anyone she dated."

"It had nothing to do with Jerrell being black?"

She turned away from me. "Don't be absurd." She waved her hand tiredly. "Did you find anything?"

I found that your stepdaughter lived a really sterile existence in this house.

"I have some leads," I said. "Are there any friends of Alais's you think she might be with?"

"I called the ones I know. They're all away at school or out of the country. I found this in Wendell's computer. It's her credit card accounts."

She handed me a computer printout. I put it in my bag.

"Thank you, that's very helpful," I said.

"Will you be evacuating?" she asked.

"I'll decide later."

"We won't be leaving for Baton Rouge until late tomorrow night. I won't leave without Alais."

"I'll do my best to find her before then, but I can't promise I'll be successful."

She turned away from me. "I know." She sounded exhausted. "I know I should call the police, but Cordelia won't hear of it."

I sat in the chair opposite hers.

"Why doesn't Cordelia want Alais talking to the police? What is she afraid she'll say?"

"Nothing."

"Does it make sense that Cordelia would have wiped your gun clean of prints before using it on Wendell?"

"I've told you before, Cordelia doesn't confide in me."

I gave up. She wasn't going to tell me anything useful. The only person who could was Alais. All I had to do was find her.

I stood up.

"I'll be in touch. I assume you'll take my calls now?"

She waved her hand again. "Of course."

I shook my head and walked out of the house.

CHAPTER EIGHT

WITH ALL DUE RESPECT to the Sheehans, self-preservation was more of a priority than finding Wendell's killer or Alais.

Had it only been three years since Paige called me in hysterics that horrible Sunday morning and told me to get out of town? I remembered the tense eight hours it took to cross the lake to Slidell, the bumper-to-bumper traffic, the cars pulled over on the shoulder so dogs could be walked. I'd fled to Dallas, driving nonstop because there were no hotel rooms available, and stayed with a guy I was seeing. We'd watched the levees fail and floods from the storm-surge annihilate the city on TV. Now it was happening again.

The whole city was being boarded up as I drove from the Sheehan house to Rouse's supermarket on Tchoupitoulas. Lawn furniture and plants were brought in. Cars were loaded with suitcases and possessions deemed too important to be left behind. Every gas station had a line. According to the radio, I-10 was already heavy with traffic out of the city and hotels were reporting no vacancies; the nearest rooms available were in Lake Charles, and those were going fast. Businesses all over the city were closing early. The radio announcer felt certain that mandatory evacuation would to be called at any moment. The last coordinates of Ginevra still indicated a direct hit on New Orleans. The National Hurricane Center said that the Category 3 storm had moved past Cuba and was now in the warm Gulf waters, leaving devastation and death in its wake. It was predicted to strengthen to Category 5 by nightfall. The Army Corps of Engineers was silent about what the levees could withstand—which told me all I needed to know on that subject.

I was still hoping I wouldn't have to evacuate, that Ginevra would change course for western Louisiana or the Florida panhandle. But even if she did, I needed to be prepared for losing power. Usually fairly empty on a weekday afternoon, Rouse's was a zoo. The parking lot was full and the aisles were jammed with people. I managed to get the last two loaves of bread, two cases of bottled water, canned meat, and other nonperishables, remembering to grab a manual can opener and hoping it was enough. Batteries and candles were long gone. Who had got there so early and bought them all? I waited in the checkout line for nearly an hour, along with the other grim, determined shoppers. The air of controlled hysteria was almost palpable. To quell my own panic, I made a list of what needed to be done when I got home: Empty the refrigerator. Fill the bathtub and sinks with water. Gather birth certificate, passport, car papers, and bankbooks, in case evacuation becomes necessary. Take as much clothing as will fit in the trunk and backseat of the car. With luck, the batteries I had on hand were still good.

Meanwhile, Rouse's employees boarded up the store's windows.

I spent another hour in line at the Shell station at Magazine and Jackson, waiting to fill up my tank. I'd had the oil changed a month ago, so that was good to go. When I was finally ready to head home, I remembered that it might not be safe to return to my apartment.

I pulled over to the Rue de la Course coffee shop on the corner of Magazine and Race, called Abby and asked her to meet me.

A couple of guys were boarding up the windows in preparation for the arrival of Ginevra. The older one, in his late thirties, fitted the plywood, and the younger guy hammered nails into the corners. Across the street, a young couple loaded their car trunk with suitcases. Farther down, an older woman applied masking tape Xs to her windows, unaware that it was a myth that this could prevent breakage.

I sat at a table outside the coffee shop, the only patron. While I waited for Abby to arrive I called Venus for an update, but got her voice mail. I tried Blaine, with the same result. Then I called Paige, who said I could stay at her place. I'd slept on her couch plenty of times in the past, and already had keys to her apartment. I was smoking my first cigarette in four years when Abby's battered Oldsmobile appeared.

Ignoring the parking meter, Abby locked the car and crossed the few yards of cement to join me. Her hair was pulled back into a ponytail, her face free of makeup. She was wearing a ratty Jazz Fest T-shirt; her cutoff jeans were just short of obscene.

"Let me get some coffee," she said.

I sipped my own while she went inside. Somehow the caffeine and the nicotine, combined with Abby's presence, calmed me, although the cigarette wasn't as nasty as I'd hoped it would be. In fact, it was quite good, and I was wondering why I'd quit in the first place.

I took another deep, grateful drag as Abby slid into the plastic chair opposite me. I blew the smoke away from her face. She reached over and plucked the cigarette from my fingers.

"You don't need that," she said, taking obvious pleasure in grinding it beneath her boot.

I started to protest, but stopped myself. Abby meant well—and the pack was in my car.

"Sorry," she said, her grin exposing the lie. "My grandmother died from lung cancer."

"I'm sure both of them would be interested to hear that," I replied.

Abby's grandmothers were very much alive.

"You've had quite a day, haven't you, hon?" she said, changing the subject. "Are you okay?"

"I'm not doing badly, all things considered."

It wasn't entirely untrue. I'd been a cop for two years before leaving the NOPD to open my own business, and I'd been shot at more than once. I'd even killed a couple of thugs who wanted to put me in the ground. But you never get used to it. The adrenaline had worn off and I was exhausted. My joints ached and my mind was fatigued. And on top of all that, I had to deal with another potentially devastating hurricane.

Abby looked at my list of things to do.

"Are you going to evacuate?" she asked.

"I'll decide Sunday morning," I said. "What about you?"

"We're staying. Our neighborhood didn't flood last time, so as long as Ginevra comes in the same way, in a worst-case scenario we'll be all right. If it comes up the river . . . There's an attic, and we have an ax to cut our way out."

"I wish you and Jeph would leave," I said.

"Where would we go? We won't abandon Rhett and Greta, and no hotel will take us with two ancient golden retrievers. Besides, there's no way we can get both dogs in the Oldsmobile, big as it. There's no sense worrying about it until we have to. I'm freaked out enough already. Why court a nervous breakdown?"

"I'd feel a lot better if I knew the two of you were going."

Abby grabbed my hands across the table.

"It'll turn, Chanse. Ginevra won't come here."

"That's what we said about Katrina."

"I know. But what can you do? After Katrina, I figured

it wouldn't happen again for a long, long time. It pisses me off."

She slurped her iced coffee noisily, as if trying to distract herself.

"Florida gets pounded every year," I reminded her.

"It's not fair," she said. She sounded like a little girl.

We sat quietly, absorbed in thought, oblivious to the racket of fleeing traffic and nails being pounded into boards. Against all odds, the city had been dragging itself back together since the last natural disaster. We were managing to live our lives day by day if not exactly triumph over the elements. Now it was all threatened again, and this time we might never recover.

I had to get us out of this mood.

"Did you have any luck with Jerrell's family, Abby?"

She welcomed the return to work.

"Did I ever! I talked to his mother, Dinah Perrilloux. You'll never guess who her aunt is—Vernita Jefferson."

"The Sheehans' housekeeper?"

"One and the same. Dinah used to work at the house whenever her aunt needed help. She couldn't have sung the Sheehans' praises higher. They paid for her to go to college, and now she's an accountant. Apparently 'Mister Wendell' offered a twenty-thousand-dollar reward for information leading to Jerrell's killer. It was almost sickening to listen to her go on about how wonderful they were. I asked her if Jerrell had any girlfriends. All she knew was that he was dating some girl in Oxford, but not her name. Then Vernita showed up. She wasn't happy to see me. She gave me the bum's rush."

"Look into that reward offer, Abby. See if people wanting the reward go through the police department, or if they had to go through Wendell. If Wendell was behind the murder, he could stonewall."

Abby typed into her Blackberry.

"I'll see what I can find out."

"Any progress on Alais's myspace?"

"Jephtha was breaking into her computer when I left the house. She had some credit card websites book-marked. Once he figures out her passwords, finding her will be a snap. Alais is a rich girl. She didn't run away to hang out with gutterpunks or go to a shelter, and she didn't take her car with her. She's checked into a hotel and it will show up on one of her cards. The hotels are giving their guests until tomorrow to get out. Alais will either have to go home or call someone."

"Put yourself in her place for a minute, Abby. You're a few years older than Alais. You've been depressed all summer because your boyfriend died. Why would you run away *now*?"

"I don't have anything in common with her, but let me think."

She leaned her chair backward and closed her eyes.

"How does this sound, boss? Alais was using the house as an escape, a kind of sanctuary where she could keep the world at arm's length while she dealt with Jerrell's death. Maybe she suspected that Wendell was responsible and on Monday night she found out for sure—and killed him."

Why hadn't it occurred to me before? I'd been so

certain it was Cordelia or Janna that it never entered my mind. Alais was in the house, and she had access to the gun. And it fit with what Carey had told me.

"That would explain why Cordelia and Janna don't want the police looking for her. I think Janna and Cordelia really don't like each other—it's not possible they faked it all these years—but they've been *using* their mutual loathing to distract everyone from the truth. Cordelia's no fool. She *had* to know picking up the gun and firing it would focus the cops on her. She came up with the cover story when Wendell killed Roger Palmer . . . Can you get on the Internet with your phone?"

Abby looked at me like I'd gone strange, probably wondering what that had to do with our discussion.

"Of course I can, but . . ."

"Find out what the hours for the Allegra Gallery are on Fridays."

She typed at her phone with her thumbs, obviously puzzled.

"It's open till nine today. What's up, boss?"

"I want to know if Cordelia had anything to do with the story about Grace Sheehan *falling* down a staircase to her death. I think Kenneth Musgrave might know the answer.

"You go home now, Abby. See if Jeph's made any progress on Alais's computer. Check out her friends on myspace."

"What are you going to do about your apartment? I thought that was why you called me. Did you get a hold of Venus?"

"I left a message on her voice mail. Whoever shot at me isn't going to give up after one attempt."

"Do you need a place to crash? You're welcome to stay with me and Jephtha."

"Thanks for the offer. I'm staying with Paige. But I need to get things from my apartment. If the shooter is still watching, he probably knows my car. I'd be a sitting duck, waiting for the electric gate to open."

"Let me do it for you. He won't recognize my Oldsmobile. You can give me the gate remote and I can go in through the back door."

"I don't like sending you into danger, Abby. Besides, I know what I need. I can put my hands on it right away."

"I can handle it, boss. Just tell me what to get. It can't be that much."

I thought out loud. "I need clothes, in case we have to evacuate. I can't leave town with just what I'm wearing. I need to transfer everything on my computer to my laptop."

"Then ride with me and hide in the backseat. I'll crouch in the driver's seat, take you to the back steps, out of firing range, park where the fence blocks me from view, then back up your files onto a flash drive while you grab everything else."

Abby really likes covert operations. Maybe I was being paranoid and it wasn't necessary, but it's better to be prepared. And I had my extra gun with me.

"Please, Chanse," she said.

"You go and work the case, Abby. I can handle this myself."

"But—"

Bless her persistence.

"No *buts*, Abby. If someone is trying to kill me, I can't spend the rest of my life hiding in your backseat. But tell you what—why don't you scope out the park and text me if you think the coast is clear. Pay particular attention to the house on the corner of Coliseum and Terpsichore. I'll wait here until I hear from you. You can stay and cover me when I get there. If someone tries to shoot me, you can spot them."

"I wish I'd brought my gun."

"My extra's in the armrest between the front seats. Help yourself."

I handed her my car keys.

As she leaned into the car, what there was of her shorts rode up. I looked away until I heard the door shut.

"Text you in a bit," she said when she returned the keys.

"Don't shoot anyone, Abby," I said with a smile, trying to lighten the mood.

She blew me a juicy raspberry. "I'm not an idiot, boss."

She sauntered toward her Oldsmobile, then turned back.

"I almost forgot. Wendell *was* at the Delacroix on Monday night. He had dinner with a Monica Davis. She got there first, had a few drinks she paid for with a credit card. They sat at a back table. The bartender didn't know anything else. The place was busy and he didn't pay attention."

"Good work, Abby."

I made a mental note to call Monica Davis, and watched until the Oldsmobile was out of sight, feeling a lot better. I wasn't going to be stupid—it still made sense to stay at Paige's for a day or two or until the evacuation, whichever came first—but at the same time I had work to do. And I had no idea whether someone was trying to kill me. There was no reason for anybody in the Sheehan family to get rid of me—none that I could figure, at any rate. Barbara was mad at me for looking into her past, but if she was angry enough to want me dead she wouldn't have told me the truth about Roger's death. She would have just fired me and showed me the door.

It was probably some weird coincidence. What else could it be?

I hated coincidences.

My cell phone beeped. Abby's message read: *Coast lks clr 2 me.*

I live in a two-story Victorian house divided into six apartments, built shortly after the Civil War. Alongside my fuchsia-colored building is a fenced-in parking area with a driveway that leads to an electronic gate. The fence is cinderblock. I hit the remote as I approached, and the gate began to rumble open. I could see Abby sitting on a low branch of a massive live oak tree, looking down at her phone with an odd expression on her face. I turned in to the driveway and the gate rolled shut behind me. The only other car in the parking area was a tired Corolla that belonged to my upstairs neighbor, Wendy. Some boxes and blankets and a suitcase stuffed the Corolla's open trunk. As I inserted the key into my back door, I heard bumping noises on the curved exterior staircase that led to Wendy's apartment.

"Hey Chanse," she said when saw me. She was dragging a suitcase behind her.

Wendy was a senior at Loyola University, majoring in anthropology. She'd been living in the tiny studio apartment at the top of the staircase since her sophomore year. She'd dated a steady stream of young men during the time I'd known her, some of whom I'd met in passing. None of them ever seemed to last long. I liked Wendy. She had a good head on her shoulders, and studied and played hard. She worked in a coffee shop on Magazine Street.

"Evacuating already?" I asked, pushing my door inward.

"My parents hounded me until I agreed to come to Chattanooga. Loyola's president canceled classes next week, and the coffee shop is closing, so I might as well go see them. I'd rather be boiled in oil, but I don't want to be here if the hurricane hits, and I don't have money to camp out in a hotel for a week. Gus told me you had some excitement this morning. Maybe it's a good time for me to get out of here, anyway."

"Have a good trip, Wendy."

I heard the Corolla chug off as I set about gathering things in my silent apartment: a change of clothes, socks, underwear, T-shirts, jeans, batteries, my shaving kit. While the computer copied my files onto a flash drive, I put my important documents into a briefcase, including my Sheehan files and Wendell's autopsy report. Wendell *had* been drunk. Janna hadn't lied about that, at least. Everything just about fit in my car with my earlier purchases.

I did an Internet directory search for Monica Davis's phone number, hoping she hadn't already left town. I was leaving my information on her voice mail when I heard knocking at the front door. I grabbed my gun from the desk drawer, crept along the side of the house to the gate, and aimed at the two men standing on my front porch. I recognized one of them from Abby's photo.

"Who are you and what do you want?" I said threateningly.

They raised their hands in the air.

"Please put the gun down, Mr. MacLeod. We're Federal agents."

They looked the part, with their dark suits over white shirts, buzz cuts and reflector sunglasses.

"Toss me your ID," I ordered.

They glanced at each other, then reached inside their jackets and tossed their leather wallets at my feet. Keeping my eyes and gun on them, I picked one up.

I lowered the gun. What had I done to warrant watching by U.S. Marshals?

"Come on in, have a seat." I unlocked the front door. "Can I offer you something to drink?"

They shook their heads no.

"I'm Special Agent Palladino," said the one with dark hair. "This is my partner, Special Agent Harrison."

We shook hands.

"I assume this isn't a social call," I said, sitting at my desk and tossing their badges to them.

"I'm afraid not, Mr. MacLeod," Palladino answered. "We're here strictly as a courtesy. If our superior knew we were talking to you, we'd be in trouble."

Harrison, the red-haired agent, started to say something, but closed his mouth at a glance from Palladino.

"I'm not following you," I said.

"Several years ago, you encountered a professional killer named Vinnie Castiglione. Do you remember him?"

I'd known him as Zane Rathburn, and he'd been very good at what he did. He was a master of disguise, assuming other people's identities and getting close to his victims. Once the victim was dead, he'd disappear without a trace. He'd been contracted to kill a New Orleans judge presiding over an organized crime case. I'd put the pieces together and proved he killed a member of the judge's family. He had successfully passed himself off as a gay man in his early twenties, and fooled me and a lot of other people for a long time. There was no telling how many deaths he'd been responsible for during the course of his career. As I recalled, Federal prosecutors cut a deal with him, in exchange for his bringing down a bunch of organized crime figures. It had galled me at the time. No matter how hard they tried to convince me—and Venus and Blaine—that it was "for the greater good," we hadn't bought it. Vinnie Castiglione was a killing machine. If anyone deserved the death penalty, it was he. At the very least, Vinnie belonged behind bars.

"I thought Vinnie was in the witness protection program," I said.

"He was," said Palladino. "He disappeared several weeks ago."

"I suppose it's too much to hope that some bad guys tracked him down and fitted him for cement shoes."

"Some people never really adjust to the program," Harrison said apologetically.

"As I recall, at the time I told you people it was a mistake."

I didn't try to hide my sarcasm.

"I appreciate your attitude more than you know, Mr. MacLeod," Palladino said blandly. "We didn't make that decision. We just did our job. Castiglione didn't fit the program at all. He complained constantly. He argued with one of his neighbors about the dog barking. The day Vinnie disappeared, the neighbor's wife came home from shopping and found the dog—and her husband—dead in the backyard, killed execution-style. And Vinnie was gone."

Palladino handed me a piece of folded paper from one of his jacket pockets. It was a computer printout of a wall covered with newspaper articles and photographs from the *Times-Picayune* and culled from online news websites—all about me.

"He's the one who shot at me this morning," I said. "He's in New Orleans and he's after me. That's why you've been watching my apartment."

"We had a tip that he's in New Orleans, and we've been trying to keep an eye on you for the past few days. He has a grudge against you, Mr. MacLeod. A grudge that's turned into an obsession. We found his fingerprints in a house on the other side of the park. He holed up there for at least a week."

My temper flared. "And you waited until now to warn me? I guess I should consider myself lucky he missed this morning!"

"He's been flushed out of his hiding place. He's probably long gone."

"You think he's evacuated?" I asked rhetorically. "He wouldn't want to get wet in all that rain. Somehow, I don't feel reassured."

"We're going to catch him, Mr. MacLeod—you don't need to worry about that. I'm sure you're safe now. But we think it might be a good idea for you to lie low for a few days."

I opened the front door. "Get out of my house," I said.

I slammed the door behind them as they left.

If I'd noticed the U.S. Marshals staking out my house, Vinnie couldn't have missed them. They were camped practically beneath the windows where he was hiding.

And if Abby could tell they were Feds, Vinnie sure as hell knew.

So why did he wait until this morning to take a shot?

I didn't believe that Vinnie Castiglione had left town. He would keep trying until he got another chance. I had to be on my guard.

Fuck, fuck, fuck.

I texted Abby to go home.

CHAPTER NINE

THE FRONT WINDOWS WERE already boarded over, and someone was optimistically writing *Ginevra go away!* in spray paint on one of them, when I arrived at Allegra Gallery. A soft, round man with a reddish face and graying hair brushed in a futile attempt to cover a deeply receding hairline supervised a staff crating prints. He wore a seersucker suit over a pale blue shirt topped with a dark blue bowtie.

"I'm looking for Kenneth Musgrave," I said as I approached them.

The man interrupted what he was doing.

"I'm Kenneth Musgrave," he said, looking up. His eyes were watery and his skin looked damp, despite the frigid air-conditioning. "How can I help you?"

"My name is Chanse MacLeod. I've been hired by Cordelia Sheehan—"

He cut me off. "Come to my office."

He asked a reedy blonde with severe black glasses to take over, and gestured for me to follow him.

"Have a seat," he said.

He poured two glasses of wine from an open bottle on a gold tray perched on a bureau behind his desk, beside a seersucker fedora. He handed me one and downed the other, then poured himself a second glass.

"Mrs. Sheehan hired me to look into her son's death," I said, holding the glass in my right hand without drinking.

He polished off his second glass, poured a third, and settled into his chair behind the desk. He leaned forward on his elbows, perspiring a bit at the hairline.

"The son of a bitch murdered my sister," he said, staring into the wine. "I suppose it's okay to say it now, him being dead and all. I won't be mourning that bastard."

It was a peculiar opening gambit for a conversation with a stranger, and it made me suspicious.

"I was under the impression your sister died in a fall down the stairs," I said, keeping my voice neutral.

"It was no accident. Wendell threw her down those stairs. I warned Grace . . ." He cleared his throat. "I saw her that afternoon. She was going to leave him."

Apparently, he'd been waiting for a chance to mouth off about his sister's death for quite some time. I let the silence grow between us, to see if he would rush in and fill it, glancing around to see what five thousand per month can do.

Kenneth Musgrave's office reeked of expensive. The soft leather armchair I'd sunk into probably cost more than all the furniture in my apartment. If his huge desk wasn't an antique, it was a costly reproduction. Black-

and-white prints of swamp scenes in gold frames hung meticulously spaced at exact distances from each other on the emerald green walls. A flat-screen monitor, computer keyboard, and black multi-line business phone sat lonely on the otherwise bare desktop, their only company a little golden tray with business cards neatly stacked in a way to discourage taking one, precariously close to the edge nearest me. There were no papers or folders anywhere in evidence.

Musgrave drummed his fingertips on the desk, getting more and more agitated with each silent, passing second.

"She should never have married him," he said finally. "Our mother was against it. She thought Grace was making a terrible mistake, and she was right. Our mother had been part of that world. Grace was forced into it growing up, and she hated it."

"Politics?" I asked.

"New Orleans society. The balls, the *right* charities. All of that nonsense that means so much to people in the Garden District. Grace thought the Sheehans weren't part of it, that it was just politics. She believed in Wendell. She wanted to help him. I think she believed they could end up in the White House. Wendell certainly thought they would."

"And you weren't part of that world? The Garden District society?"

"We had different fathers. Our mother was a Caldwell."

"Okay," I said. The name meant nothing to me, although he seemed to think it would.

"After Grace's father died, our mother married my father"—his already reddish face flushed a bit—"a nobody accountant from Metairie. It was social suicide. But they loved each other, and they were happy. Her parents never forgave her."

I noted that he referred to their maternal grandparents as *her parents*.

"Grace inherited a lot of money from her father, and *her* bloodlines were impeccable. The crime of our mother's second marriage wasn't held against her. She was Queen of Rex, you know—Grace's grandparents on both sides pushed her into New Orleans society while excluding our mother."

Unspoken but implied were the words *and me*.

"Grace hated all the balls and parties, but our mother thought she should do them. She was twenty when she married Wendell Sheehan. She had Alais a year or so later. It was a tough pregnancy, and afterward she couldn't have another child. That's when the marriage went south."

"Then why did she stay?"

"She loved him, I suppose. She never said anything against Wendell, but I could see she wasn't happy. There were other women. Wendell didn't keep it a secret. Grace didn't seem to care about that. If it was good enough for Hillary Clinton, I think Grace felt she could put up with it. She focused her energies on Alais."

"So, after all those years, why did she finally decide to leave him?"

He emptied the glass and rolled the stem between his fingers.

"I'm not sure. We had lunch that day at Galatoire's. That's when she told me she was taking Alais and leaving him. She'd rented herself an apartment and was meeting with a divorce attorney that afternoon. When I asked her why, she said she'd finally had enough. She didn't want anything from the Sheehans. The money her father left her was more than enough for her to live on the rest of her life. She just wanted out. I told her Wendell might not want a divorce. He was attorney general then, and he was pretty open about running for governor in the next election cycle. She said Wendell had two choices: a quiet divorce or a long, drawn-out ugly one for adultery. I thought she was bluffing. Surely she didn't want the whole world to know her business. She left Galatoire's to meet with her lawyer—and died that night. You do the math."

"You don't have any proof?"

He smiled slyly. "I know what I know."

"Enough to blackmail him?"

I pulled out the photocopies of Wendell's checks from my bag and tossed them on the desk. His face turned scarlet as he shuffled through the papers.

"I wasn't blackmailing him."

"Then what were the checks for?"

He slid them back to me across the desk.

"Grace left me a trust in her will. Wendell controlled it. I'd had some problems when I was younger, and

Grace set it up that way because she was afraid I'd go through the money if I had it. Wendell invested it and paid me the monthly interest on the principle."

But the checks hadn't been drawn on a trust account. They were from a discretionary account.

"It'll be very easy to check into that, you know."

"Are you calling me a liar?"

"Merely pointing out a fact," I said. "It is a murder investigation, after all."

He shifted in his seat.

"What's to investigate? Cordelia shot him."

"There's some question about that. That's why she hired me."

"Of course she'll get away with it," he said dismissively. "The Sheehans get away with everything. They're a law unto themselves." He flashed a nasty smile. "The law is for the common people."

"Like you?"

"He got away with killing my sister, didn't he?"

"You seem so certain Grace was murdered."

He glared at me.

"Alais saw the whole thing. She heard them arguing and opened her bedroom door. Grace came out of her room and Wendell pursued her. He grabbed her at the top of the stairs and started slapping her. She tried to get away. Finally he picked her up and threw her down the stairs. She broke her neck."

"Alais told you this?"

He spun his chair around, grabbed the wine bottle, and refilled his glass.

"We used to be close. When I heard about Grace, I went over there. Alais was . . . Neither Wendell nor Cordelia seemed much concerned about her. She wouldn't talk to anyone. It took me a while, but I was able to get the story out of her. She was only eight years old, poor kid."

"And rather than going to the police, you decided to blackmail Wendell. Might I ask why you sold yourself so cheaply?"

He couldn't look me in the eyes.

"That wasn't what the money was for. Wendell collected art. He paid me to find pieces for him."

That was a lie. I'd gotten a look at some of the work still on display in the gallery. There was no way Cordelia Sheehan would allow abstract art on her precious walls.

"Then where did you get the money for this place?"

He was unable to keep from smiling.

"Wendell released the trust."

"And you promised not to tell anyone what Alais witnessed the night her mother died."

I didn't try to veil my contempt.

"It was my money," he said. "Grace had left it to me. I always wanted to run a gallery. It was my dream. But I could never come up with the money. When I was younger, I did a lot of stupid things—drugs, alcohol— things I now regret. That's why Grace wouldn't back the gallery. It made me angry, but I understood. She was afraid I'd blow it."

"And when Alais told you how her mother died, you saw that as an opportunity to get what you wanted."

"Like I said, it was my money. If she'd lived, eventually

Grace would have backed the gallery. I really believe that."

It was getting hard to control my disgust. All I could think of was Alais, an eight-year-old child who'd witnessed her father kill her mother, and her uncle using the information to extort money from him. What a house of horrors to grow up in. No wonder she'd finally run away.

"It must have been difficult for you, being an outcast while your wealthy older sister was welcomed into society."

"It wasn't fair. My mother was a *Caldwell*, and her parents—my grandparents—never acknowledged me. Not one birthday, no Christmas presents, nothing. My father felt terrible about how they treated me and my mother. But they couldn't do enough for Grace. When they died, they left everything to her."

"You said you were no longer close to Alais. Why was that?"

"After—"

He picked up the wine glass and carefully put it back down. He had the decency to sound ashamed.

"One of the conditions of Wendell releasing the trust was that I no longer be a part of Alais's life."

"You sold out your eight-year-old niece—the daughter of the sister you say you loved—for this gallery."

"For my dream."

I stood up.

"One last question. Where were you on Monday night?"

"I was here all night. Now get out of my office. I have work to do."

With pleasure, I thought angrily.

I slammed the door behind me. The reedy woman looked at me curiously as I strode through the gallery, but I ignored her. I was heading for my car when she caught up to me.

"Mr. MacLeod, was it?"

"That's right. And you are?"

"Meredith Cole." She smiled, and her entire face changed.

Meredith Cole was tall and almost excessively thin. Her tight black wool dress left little to the imagination, but flattered her slender, long-legged figure. She had no curves to speak of. Her blonde hair was pulled back in a tight chignon, and she wore minimal makeup above the simple gold chain around her neck. She glanced back at the gallery door, and her smile faded.

"Ken wasn't here Monday night, if that's what he told you." She flushed. "I don't want to cause any trouble. I know this is none of my business. But Tuesday morning, Ken ordered me to tell anyone who asked about it that he was here all night on Monday."

"And he wasn't?"

She shook her head. "I was here until almost midnight, catching up on the books—by myself. And when I saw the news—"

She continued "Wendell Sheehan came to the gallery on Monday morning and they argued, I don't know what about. Ken was in a really bad mood after he left. Nothing anyone did was right. I almost quit."

"Had Wendell ever come by before?"

"Not that I recall, other than openings. I got the impression Ken didn't like him much. Wendell was always almost rude to him, if you know what I mean. Ken doesn't take that from anyone, but he always took it from Wendell. I assumed Wendell was one of his backers."

"Ken said that he procured art for Wendell."

"I keep the books and do the billing. Wendell Sheehan never bought a thing from us."

My cell phone rang.

"I need to get back," she said, glancing over her shoulder. She slipped her business card into my hand. "My cell number is on there—if you have any more questions."

I thanked her, and answered my phone.

"This is Monica Davis. I'm returning your call?"

I waited for the gallery door to close before I responded.

"I'm a private investigator. I was wondering if I could come by and ask you some questions?"

"That's what you said in your message. I've been racking my brain trying to figure out why you want to talk to me. My dinner plans just canceled, so if you want to come by now, I shouldn't be too drunk. Here's my address."

I promised to be right there, and headed uptown.

There was no traffic on St. Charles. At Calliope, cars

were backed up as far as I could see, all the way from the highway on-ramp. I dialed WWL for news.

The latest report from the National Hurricane Center showed Ginevra at Category 4, predicted to strengthen to Category 5 in a few hours, with a high probability of New Orleans taking a direct hit. A lot of people weren't waiting for the mandatory evacuation order. Traffic was at a standstill on I-10, and highway patrol projected a five- to six-hour drive to Baton Rouge. Hotels along the route were booked as far as Houston. An hour ago, the mayor had called a press conference to announce that the city and state had arranged bus transportation for those without the means to evacuate on their own, and urged everyone to leave as soon as possible. The National Guard were airlifting hospital patients out of the city, and the governor had stated that anyone planning to ignore the mandatory evacuation order when it came should expect no assistance or rescue.

I turned off the radio. The other side of St. Charles was clogged with cars, but in the uptown direction I was pretty much the only driver. Businesses were closed, windows boarded up. It was so strange—there were no clouds, the sun was shining, and the sky itself was an amazing shade of blue. It was a beautiful day, yet deadly winds, flooding rains, death and destruction moved inexorably towards the city. I tried to remember the days before the last evacuation, but like everything pre-Katrina, the memories were foggy and unclear. I gave up. The situation was depressing enough without dwelling on it.

Monica Davis lived on Dante Street in Riverbend, a nice, quiet neighborhood with streets lined with massive live oak trees arching like canopies over the pavement. The area was named for a near-ninety-degree turn in the Mississippi River, past the universities and Audubon Park where St. Charles Avenue ends and the streetcar line makes a ninety-degree turn onto Carrollton. I rarely made it that far uptown. Her house was on a corner lot, a small bungalow-style building with a covered carport, beneath which a white Lexus was parked. I pulled in front of the house. There were very few cars anywhere. Everything was eerily silent.

A short woman answered the door, holding a drink in her left hand.

"Chanse MacLeod, I presume?"

Monica Davis was maybe five feet tall, and couldn't have weighed more than ninety pounds. Apparently Wendell Sheehan liked his women short. She was wearing a green and white nylon jogging suit with the Tulane emblem across the chest. Her dirty blonde hair was cut short in a bob, with an occasional strand of gray here and there. Her only makeup was a touch of lipstick and maybe something around her eyes. She looked to be in her forties and was aging gracefully. As she unlatched the screen to let me in, I saw that she was in her stocking feet.

Her small, square living room was painted pale blue. The low ceiling made me a bit claustrophobic. The furniture looked lived-in and chosen for comfort rather than fashion. There was no television, but the stereo was softly playing a recording of Pachelbel's Canon.

"Thank you for agreeing to see me," I said. "I appreciate it."

"What else do I have to do, listen to doom and gloom on the radio? Please, have a seat."

She sat down in a rocking chair and rattled the ice in her drink at me.

"Can I offer you something? I'm having Kahlua and cream. If you prefer it, I have vodka and some Abita Light. Or a soft drink."

"I'm fine, thank you."

I sat down on the couch. There wasn't enough room for my legs between the couch and the coffee table, so I turned slightly sideways and crossed them.

"Are you going to join the mass exodus?" she asked.

"Right now, I plan on waiting," I said. "There's still a chance it could turn, right?"

The truth was, I was hoping that if I waited long enough Ginevra would turn and I wouldn't have to leave town.

"I'm not going," she said. "I know it's crazy, but after the last time I swore I wouldn't ever leave again. I'm afraid if I do I won't come back, or I won't be able to come back. I don't want to be anywhere else."

That was exactly how I felt.

"We were able to come back last time."

"If the levees fail again? I don't think so. Plenty of people the last time thought we shouldn't have been helped, that the city should just be allowed to die. If it happens again, this soon, there will be even more who feel that way. And what if it comes up the river this time? Do you think the river levees will hold?"

She rocked slowly in the chair.

After Katrina, the whole focus had been on the levees around the lake and the canals that fed the lake. No one really talked about the whether the river levees would hold. The truth was, if the Katrina surge had come up the river instead of through the lake, the Mississippi would have overtopped its levees and destroyed the city in a completely different way—down in the lower ninth ward. That's what had happened in 1965, during Hurricane Betsy.

"A storm surge up the river wouldn't make it this far," I said.

"So, there's no reason for me to leave, other than creature comforts like air-conditioning. Now then, Mr. Chanse MacLeod, what did you want to talk to me about? I've never had a private eye want to grill me before. Please, tell me before I die of suspense."

"I've been hired by Cordelia Sheehan to look into her son's death."

She held the glass to the side of her face and closed her eyes.

"Ironically, that was the one possibility that never crossed my mind. I suppose it was inevitable, since I was one of the last people to see him alive that night. I'm surprised the police haven't come sniffing around."

"You had dinner with Wendell at the Delacroix."

She opened her eyes.

"You're quite good. Yes, I had dinner with him that night. It was a mistake. I pride myself on my intelligence, and that was a stupid thing to do. But sometimes you can't help picking at scabs."

"Whose idea was it?"

"Wendell's. He called me Monday afternoon. I was so shocked, I didn't know what to say. I hadn't talked to him in almost five—no, seven years now. We didn't part on the best of terms. He wanted to talk to me about something, but he wouldn't say what on the phone. I figured he wanted help on his Senate campaign. I'd worked on both of his City Council campaigns, and his run for attorney general. The only one I didn't work on was the campaign for mayor—and look how that turned out. I was curious, so I went. If I didn't like his pitch, I'd say no and walk out."

"But it wasn't about the campaign?"

"Yes and no. That's one thing about Wendell—he was unpredictable. Maybe that's what attracted me to him in the first place. Don't look surprised. You knew we had dinner together. Obviously you've done your homework. But that was ancient history. He wanted to talk about Alais."

This genuinely surprised me.

"Alais? Were you close to her?"

"Not really. She was always around during the campaigns. I thought she was a sweet little girl. I liked Grace too. We got along well."

"Did she know about you and Wendell?"

"She knew Wendell was unfaithful, but did she know

I was one of his women? We never talked about it. She didn't strike me as a woman who would be friendly to a woman sleeping with her husband, but who knows?"

"Why did Wendell want to talk to you about Alais?"

"You know, I asked him that very question. Do you mind if I smoke?"

"Do you mind if I grub one?"

She pulled a pack of cigarettes from her pocket, handed me one, lit her own, then passed the lighter to me.

"It's shocking how many people are outraged when I smoke in my own home and pollute their air."

She blew the smoke out.

"Actually, I quit a couple of years ago," I said. "But the last few days I've felt the need."

"It never goes away. That's why ex-smokers are so self-righteous. Anyway, Wendell was worried about Alais. Apparently some boy she'd been seeing up at school was murdered. He wanted my opinion. I told him, 'Talk to your wife.' He said she was useless, all she wanted was to coddle the girl, let her mope around her room. He thought Alais needed to get on with her life. I told him, 'Jesus Christ, Wendell, she's a teenager and it's only been a few months. She thinks her life is over. Give her time and she'll snap out of it.' He was an asshole. What did I ever see in him?"

"That was all you two talked about?"

"That was his opening gambit. He thought talking about his daughter's problems would make me more sympathetic, make me feel sorry for him. That kind of thing used to work on me. But when he asked me to run his campaign, I told him, 'No way in hell,' and that was that. He wasn't happy about it—he's used to getting his way. All through dinner, he kept trying to convince me. In the seven years since we ended things, he hadn't changed. He was still the same jackass."

"Was he going home when he left the Delacroix?"

"That's what he said. I don't know if he did or not."

"Did he drink with dinner?"

"Wendell always drank. I'd heard that he stopped after Grace died, but I didn't believe it."

"Do you think he had a drinking problem?"

"Kind of hard to tell in New Orleans, isn't it?" She held up her glass. "I drink every day. Does that make me an alcoholic? Or am I just in denial?"

"So why did your relationship with Wendell end?"

"I got tired of being the other woman. I'm a feminist, Mr. MacLeod. I never wanted to get married. I never wanted children. I enjoy my life very much, and I didn't want to become Mrs. Wendell Sheehan. I don't need a man for anything other than— I almost said something unladylike. Maybe I've had enough to drink."

She put the glass down and looked away from me.

"So, you broke it off," I said.

"Wendell didn't take rejection well. He got angry. He had a terrible temper. He kept it under control in public but not in private. I told him to get out, that if necessary, I'd get a restraining order."

"Did he ever hurt you physically?"

"Wendell preferred emotional cruelty for his women. I don't think he much liked the female sex.

Not surprising, given that soulless bitch of a mother. I need another drink. Are you sure I can't get you something?"

"I could go for an Abita Light," I said. The cigarette had dried my mouth.

While Monica mixed her drink in the kitchen, my eyes wandered the room.

There were books everywhere—two overflowing bookcases, covering the dining table behind the couch (with papers and a closed laptop), on every other possible surface in the room. Mozart now played on the excellent sound system.

Monica handed me an ice-cold bottle of Abita Light, and returned to the rocker with her refresher. A cool sip eased my throat.

"You mentioned that Wendell didn't handle rejection well," I said carefully. "How would he have reacted, in your opinion, if Grace had wanted a divorce?"

"He would have gone crazy, absolutely bat-shit. But Grace didn't want a divorce."

"I was told that the afternoon she died she saw a divorce lawyer."

"Who told you that?"

"Her brother."

"Kenny? You had me going there, for a moment. That miserable little toad wouldn't know the truth if it punched him in the face."

"You know him?"

"Oh, yes. He was always around the campaigns. If a dirty trick needed to be done, Kenny was your go-to guy. When Wendell was running for attorney general, one of his strongest opponents in the primary was a law-and-order D.A. from Shreveport. He had all the machines in north Louisiana backing him, and it was going to be a tough fight. Somehow Kenny found out that this district attorney liked to have private sessions with girls whenever he was in New Orleans. Kenny got to one of them, gave her some cocaine, and then had a buddy of his on the police force raid the room. In exchange for the whole thing going away, the D.A. agreed to drop out of the race and support Wendell."

"Do you think it's possible Wendell killed Grace?"

"I know for a fact it isn't. He was with me the night she died. I was here when he got the call that they'd found her body."

"Did you know Wendell paid Kenny five thousand dollars every month after Grace died? Kenny also claims Wendell released the trust Grace created for him."

"Oh, hell. Kenny was the one who called Wendell about Grace. Maybe Kenny killed her. Maybe Wendell paid him to do it. Anything was possible with those two. All I know for sure is that Kenny Musgrave is a liar. He would do anything for money."

"Thank you for your time, Ms. Davis."

"Monica, please. Is that all you wanted to know?"

"I'm afraid so."

She looked disappointed.

"What am I going to do to entertain myself the rest of the night?"

CHAPTER TEN

"Why the hell haven't you two arrested Cordelia Sheehan?" I asked Venus and Blaine as Paige got back from the bar with our drinks.

I was only half serious.

The Rolling Stones' "Sympathy for the Devil" blared on the jukebox. Venus and Blaine exchanged glances.

"There's a lot of bullshit going on in the department with this investigation," Venus replied. "I shouldn't say anything about this, but I don't fucking care anymore."

"Some of the evidence has been"—Blaine made air quotes with his fingers—"'*misplaced*.' We're under investigation by Internal Affairs, because, *of course*, it's our fault."

"In other words, someone higher up decided to make sure Cordelia Sheehan never spends a day in jail—and we're taking the fall for it." Venus spat out the words.

Both their faces were grim.

"Twenty goddamn years I've been a cop here," Venus fumed. "I did my job during Katrina when half the cops got out of town or looted or did god knows what. They *needed* me, so like a damned fool I stayed. I've never taken a bribe or a shortcut. And now this rich white bitch kills someone, and my career is destroyed because of it? I don't need this shit. I put in for retirement this morning."

I stared at her in shock.

The four of us were sitting at a scarred table in the Avenue Pub. The windows were open. The traffic on St. Charles had lessened. Two guys whose sleeveless shirts displayed meaty biceps covered in multicolored tattoos were playing pool. A couple of people sat at the bar, where the big-screen TV hanging in a corner was tuned to the Weather Channel. Every so often I-10 West appeared on the screen, packed bumper-to-bumper with crawling cars.

Paige leapt into the breach. "I'll do a story—"

"And publish it where?" Blaine challenged. "In *Crescent City*? Yeah, and the Sheehans will give it the cover."

"I can pitch it to the *Times-Picayune*," she said.

"They won't run the story either, Paige. Cordelia Sheehan is too powerful," Venus said. "Anyway, it doesn't matter. I'm done."

I finally managed to say something.

"What about you, Blaine? What are you going to do?"

"I don't know. I'm pissed, but what am I going to do if I quit? I don't want to live off David. He doesn't like me being a cop any more than my parents do, and I know he'd be thrilled if I left the force. But I can't *not* work. I'm not interested in being *kept*."

"I told you, go back to school and get your master's," Venus admonished him, toying with the ice in her empty cup. "You're young enough to start a new career. It's too late for me, but if I sell my house, with my pension I can get a condo in Memphis. It might be nice to watch my grandkids grow up, live closer to my girls. I thought about it after the flood. Now I kind of wish I'd done it then."

"You're sure Cordelia did it?" I asked.

I was having trouble wrapping my mind around the idea of a Venus-free police department. I didn't like it one bit.

"She fired the goddamn gun. We have a witness who saw her standing over the body with it moments after the victim was shot. If she were anyone else, she'd be sitting in a cell at Central Lockup right now. And her story? Holes, holes, holes. Of course, by the time Blaine and I got there on Monday night, her lawyer was at her side."

Paige started making notes.

"What evidence is missing? How crucial is it to the case?"

"The crime scene photos are gone. Even the negatives," Blaine said. "Lifted right off Venus's desk. When we requested new copies, we found out that all copies—and the negatives—have vanished into the ether."

"But the district attorney's office doesn't *need* them to move forward," Paige persisted. "Do they?"

Venus's eyes glinted. "Guess who got the case? Evan Cochrane."

Evan Cochrane had the worst track record of any prosecutor in the district attorney's office. Rumor had it he kept his job solely due to the influence of someone at City Hall who was in the pocket of organized crime. Every defense attorney in New Orleans hoped they'd draw Cochrane, because he settled every case. I felt sorry for him when I read disparaging stories about him in the *Times-Picayune* or *Gambit Weekly*, but if I was ever charged with anything, I hoped he'd be my prosecutor.

"I'd have thought the D.A. himself would take this one on," I said.

"The district attorney has to be *elected*," Blaine sneered. "And no one in an elected office in Orleans Parish wants to take on the Sheehans."

"From day one, everything about this goddamn case has been off-kilter," Venus snapped. "If you ask me, someone's pulling strings and favors are being traded." She looked at me. "The murder weapon's also gone. At least whoever swiped our evidence left the fucking ballistics report. We may not have the gun anymore, but we know that it *was* the gun that shot Wendell Sheehan and also put a bullet into the floor. What have *you* turned up? Do you think she's innocent?"

I hesitated before answering her. Venus was, without question, the best detective on the force. Unlike the majority of her colleagues, she always kept an open mind. Once evidence against someone began to accumulate, most of them tended to stop looking at other suspects. As long as I had known Venus, she had never succumbed to that kind of laziness—but apparently her anger at all the hindrances to this investigation had closed her mind. I understood it. In her position, it would be hard not to be convinced of Cordelia's guilt. And frankly, Cordelia was paying me to keep my mind open.

"I'm not sure it was Cordelia who shot him," I said carefully. "At the same time, her story stinks to high heaven, and I can't believe a lawyer as savvy as Loren McKeithen allowed her to tell it to the cops. I don't doubt there's behind-the-scenes shenanigans going on, but I don't think this case is as simple as it appears to be."

"So if she didn't do it, who did?" Venus demanded. "Why would she pull all this shit—and ruin the careers of two good cops—if she wasn't trying to cover her tracks?"

"Did you interview Alais Sheehan?"

"Not really," Blaine answered. "She was pretty doped up that night. She said she never left her room, that she had her headphones on and didn't hear anything. We've wanted to talk to her again when she isn't zonked out on something, but she's not available."

I knew I should tell them she was missing, but I was confident that Abby would track her down.

"And Carey? The boy?"

"Same thing. See no evil, hear no evil," Venus said in disgust. "There was *no one else* in that house Monday night, Chanse. Open and shut."

She pushed back from the table and stood up.

"Anyone need another drink?"

Having no takers, she strode to the bar.

"She's not doing well," Paige said.

"I'm not doing so good myself," Blaine said. He leaned forward. "The thing is . . . the crime scene photos going missing isn't that big a deal—except for one thing. Both Cordelia and Janna Sheehan claim that Wendell came home only a few minutes before he was shot. That night the rain started around ten-thirty. He was shot at eleven-thirty. If he'd just gotten home, why was the pavement under his car dry? We got photos of it. Of course, now the photos are gone, and according to Cochrane, without them it's just our word against theirs in court, and he doesn't think *our* word is enough. He's probably right. No one in town trusts cops anyway, and *she's* Cordelia Sheehan, patron saint of abused women."

Paige scribbled away in her pad.

"Did you question Janna and Cordelia about it?"

"We'd already questioned them when it was brought to our attention, and McKeithen wouldn't let us near them again. But we didn't ask you here to bitch about the Sheehan case. This afternoon we—"

My cell phone rang. Caller ID read JEPHTHA. I excused myself and walked outside to take the call.

"What's up, Jeph?"

"Hey, Chanse, I got into Alais's computer and broke the passwords. Abby's out checking the charges on her credit cards. She's been using a MasterCard pretty heavily—always in the Quarter. I haven't found anything from hotels yet, but I haven't finished looking. I wanted to let you know about her myspace page."

He sounded excited.

"What about it?"

"Myspace has blog software as part of its service—you know, a web diary."

"I know what a blog is, Jeph," I said, annoyed. "I read one of the entries. Someone deleted the rest of them. I told Abby to have you see if you could find them."

"That entry was posted *after* the purge," he said smugly. "She backdated it. My guess is she wrote it off-line, and then posted it later. Around eleven o'clock that morning, someone purged all her blog entries. From what I can tell, she'd been keeping it for over a year. I'm about to start reconstructing them. I was just curious to know if you wanted me to do the whole thing, or to start someplace specific."

What had she written that someone felt the need to get rid of the morning after the murder? I flipped through my notepad.

"Start with anything in the last two weeks, and then go back and see what you can find in the two-week period around June fourth, when Jerrell was killed. E-mail it all to me, then reconstruct the rest and give those entries to Abby to read. Tell her to let me know if she finds anything of interest."

"I'm on it, boss."

Venus was already halfway through her next drink when I got back to the table. Paige gave me a worried look. Venus and Blaine were frowning.

"What did I miss?" I asked no one in particular.

Paige began, "Blaine was just about to tell you—"

"I'll do it," Venus interrupted, turning to me. "We got pulled off your shooting case this afternoon. Feds swarmed in and took all our notes, everything."

"Did they say why?" Paige asked.

"Like they'd bother to tell mere NOPD detectives anything," Venus scoffed.

"It's because of Vinnie Castiglione," I said, and filled them in on the U.S. Marshals' visit to my apartment.

"Maybe you *should* evacuate," Blaine said seriously. "Tonight."

"I just need to be careful. The hurricane won't reach New Orleans until Sunday night, if it comes at all, and I'm not going back to my apartment, anyway. Paige, if you don't want me to stay with you—"

"Don't be ridiculous, Chanse. My apartment is pretty secure. My windows can't be accessed by a sniper. The only way he could get in is through the front door, and before he can do that he has to climb over the fence. This morning my landlady strung razor wire along the top, to keep out looters after the evacuation—as if the walls weren't high enough to discourage them."

"I don't know, Paige. If anything happened to you because of me . . ."

"We both have guns, Chanse. We can barricade ourselves in with all the supplies you brought. Besides, it's just down the street, and Venus and Blaine can cover us."

"We'll come with you," Venus said.

"Maybe we should camp out there, too," Blaine added. "Four guns are better than two."

"You'd have to sleep on the floor," Paige pointed out. "And you aren't retired yet. You'll both be working around the clock the next few days. Chanse and I will be perfectly safe once we're inside. Discussion closed."

We walked briskly down Polymnia, on the lookout for any lurking presence. The street was ominously silent. This area of New Orleans is usually pretty noisy, what with the traffic, the clicking and clacking of streetcars along St. Charles, snatches of conversation carried on the wind, and constant music coming from all directions. It quiets down late at night, but it was still broad daylight now. Paige voiced what we were all thinking.

"It's like a scene from some end-of-the-world movie."

She pulled out her keys as we reached the intricate wrought iron fence that fronted the house. Sure enough, coils of razor wire ran all the way along the top. She unlocked the gate on the right, and we followed her past the elevated front porch and along the concrete path to her duplex at the back.

"Let's scope out the place, Chanse," Blaine suggested as Paige climbed the wooden steps the five feet to her door and fit her key into the lock.

"I'll do the same inside," Venus offered.

Blaine and I circumnavigated the house, remaining wary.

Formerly a single-family dwelling, the gigantic Victorian had been split into three generous units, each with two floors. Like all residential buildings in New Orleans, the living area was at least five feet above the ground, because of perennial flooding. Paige's landlady and her husband lived on the left side, which was separated from the property next door by a seven-foot-high stone fence with coils of razor wire across the top. A nice gay couple occupied the huge apartment that took up two-thirds of the right side, separated from the property on that side by another seven-foot stone fence, the top of which also was lined with razor wire. An unbroken line of crepe myrtle trees beyond it shaded the house. If Vinnie somehow broke into the property next door, the thickness of the crepe myrtles would prevent him from getting a clear shot into any of Paige's windows. Her living room window was covered with curtains. There was a direct line from the rear carriage house next door into the breakfast nook extending from her kitchen, but as we passed beneath the demi-hexagon we saw Venus and Paige hanging sheets over the usually exposed bay window there. Although that carriage house had no gallery, the one in the back on Paige's property did. A large patio opened off the upstairs hall between Paige's bathroom and bedroom, but there was no way to get up there except through Paige's apartment. The property on the other side also had a carriage house with a gallery, but the galleries as well were separated by razor wire.

"I worry about the patio," Blaine told Venus when we joined her and Paige again inside. "Otherwise the property is a fortress. What's the story with the neighbors, Paige?"

"John and Michael left this morning."

She uncorked a bottle of wine. "You guys want any?"

"We should be getting home," Venus said.

I walked her and Blaine to the gate. The crepe myr-tles whispered as they swayed in the slight breeze.

"Be careful, Chanse," Venus said.

"You, too," I responded.

Venus hesitated, then pulled me into a rib-cracking hug.

"Don't know when I'll see you again," she said, her voice husky with emotion, and stepped back.

I was oddly moved. In all the years I'd known her, Venus had never been an expressive person.

Blaine hugged me.

"We'll be on evacuation detail tomorrow," he said. "If you need us, call my cell. Now get into the house."

They watched me scuttle back to Paige's apartment.

Paige sat calmly on the couch, her hands shaking slightly as she rolled a joint. She toked deeply and of-fered me a hit. I shook my head. I didn't think getting stoned right now was a good idea, but I didn't say so. The television was tuned to the Weather Channel. In the French Quarter, merchants boarded up their win-dows while customers drank inside the bars.

"Can you believe this?" Paige said. "I feel this hor-rible sense of déjà vu, like I'm watching a movie I've already seen and didn't like very much the first time."

"I still can't wrap my mind around the idea that we may take another direct hit."

"Where will you go?"

"Houston, I guess. I haven't thought that far ahead."

She inhaled again, then carefully put the joint out in the ashtray.

"How is your mother doing, Chanse?" she said, looking concerned. "Really."

I opened my mouth to give my automatic response, but it wouldn't come.

"She's dying, Paige. They found the cancer too late. She ignored the signs, didn't see a doctor. She's got a couple of months left, tops."

I reached for her pack of cigarettes and lit one.

"I'm sorry, Chanse. Are you glad you went last week?"

"Yeah, I'm glad I went." I changed the subject. "Where will you go?"

"I got a reservation for Sunday at a Hilton near the Houston airport. I figure if I leave tomorrow, I won't get there until then anyway. But if you're heading that way, we should just leave together and convoy."

"What about Ryan?"

"They left a few hours ago for Atlanta. His ex has family there."

"Then why don't you go to Atlanta and be with him?"

"He asked me to marry him, Chanse."

"Paige, that's great!"

The look on her face dampened my enthusiasm.

"Don't you want to?"

"Sometimes I do, sometimes I don't. I know it's selfish, but when I marry someone, I want to be his priority, at least occasionally. I'll never be that with Ryan.

His kids come before everything—and his ex takes advantage of that at every opportunity. I *like* the kids a lot, but . . ."

"Maybe you *should* go to Atlanta, Paige."

I was hardly the person to give her advice, having pretty much blown every relationship I'd ever had.

"I think maybe this evacuation might be a good thing, Chanse. I can use the time to try and figure all of this out."

She lit the joint again and grinned at me.

"Enough of this wallowing—for both of us. I got the sense at the Avenue that the case isn't going well."

I crushed my cigarette in the ashtray.

"Alais Sheehan is missing, and the family doesn't want the police involved."

"Christ. You don't think Alais killed Wendell, do you?"

"It would explain why Janna and Cordelia are lying about what happened that night. But *why* would she kill her father? Kenneth Musgrave—her uncle—said that when she was eight years old Alais saw Wendell murder her mother. That's a motive. But why wait ten years to do it? Monica Davis warned me not to believe anything Musgrave told me."

"If Monica said that, it's true," Paige said.

"She had dinner with Wendell the night he was murdered. He wanted to talk to her about Alais. He was concerned about her depression and wanted Monica's advice on how to snap her out of it."

"Why was she depressed?"

"Her boyfriend was murdered in June, up at Ole Miss. A young black man named Jerrell Perrilloux."

"I remember that murder," Paige said. "Rachel was interested in it, but she didn't say why. She had me start to look into the story, thought it might be racially motivated. But before I got going, she pulled me off it."

"Jerrell's murder happened after Janna found out about the affair. Carey Sheehan seemed to think there was a connection. What if Wendell killed him?" It didn't sound too far-fetched, once I said it out loud. "Maybe he didn't like the idea of his daughter dating a black man."

"The Sheehans aren't racists, Chanse. Bobby Sheehan did more for civil rights in Louisiana than—"

"Maybe not publicly," I interjected, recalling my conversation with Janna. "Why else would Cordelia do something as stupid as picking up the gun and firing it, unless she were covering for Alais? Janna and Cordelia cooked up their stories, sent Alais upstairs, told her to tell the police she hadn't left her room or heard anything."

"That doesn't make sense, Chanse. A good defense lawyer could come up with a reasonable defense for Alais. I can think of three off the top of my head—it was an accident, she wasn't in her right mind, she'd been depressed all summer—and I'm not Loren McKeithen. Plus there's the Sheehan pull. Why would Cordelia take such a huge risk?"

"I doubt Cordelia and Janna cared about Alais dating a black kid, one way or the other. But they didn't want it coming out. If Wendell killed the boy, they'd do anything to protect him—and there's Alais's motive. Janna and Cordelia didn't have time to think it through."

"You're suggesting that Janna and Cordelia are not only covering for Alais, but they also *knew* Wendell killed Jerrell and were covering that up as well. Isn't that a little convoluted?"

I couldn't tell Paige that Cordelia had already covered up Roger Palmer's murder without betraying Barbara's confidence.

"If Wendell did kill his first wife—"

"But Monica told you not to believe Musgrave's story."

"Musgrave could be a liar *and* be telling the truth about that. He had something on Wendell, enough to force Wendell not only to break the trust Grace set up for Musgrave but also to pay him five grand a month after Grace died. From what I've heard about Wendell, he wouldn't have done that to be nice."

"I admit, it's a great story, Chanse, but you don't have any proof."

My cell phone interrupted us. Jephtha had just e-mailed what he'd recovered from Alais's blog, and told me to look at them right away. I pulled my laptop from my bag.

"What's going on?" Paige asked.

"Alais kept a blog on her myspace page. The morning after the murder all the entries were deleted. Jeph has been reconstructing it. Nothing ever completely disappears from the Internet."

Paige joined me on the couch as the download completed and I clicked the document open.

11 August

I don't know how much longer I can stay in this house. Nobody seems to understand how I feel, and I have nobody to talk to. With every day that passes, my suspicions make more sense to me, I am being smothered in this place. They don't allow me to see anyone, they don't allow me to talk to anyone.

I don't want to believe it. If it's true I might really lose my mind once and for all. I'm sure Mother thinks I'm overreacting, that I'm just a drama queen and want attention. She wouldn't believe me if I told her, and I know Gram wouldn't.

I'm so sorry, Jerry. I loved you, I always did. If I'd known it would turn out this way I would never have let you near me. I will always love you, my sweet Jerry.

I can't go on this way. I've been avoiding the confrontation ever since I came home. But I have to be strong. Once and for all I have to know the truth. I owe that to Jerry.

12 August

Mother is acting strange. She had an appointment this morning, and when she came back she went straight to her room. I know she hasn't been feeling well, but when I asked her this afternoon if everything was okay, she brushed me off and went back to her room and shut the door.

Gram is acting weird, too. Everyone in this house is acting weird. Or maybe it's just me.

Last night I had the nightmare again. I woke up crying and had to take one of the damned pills. Mother and Gram are so determined that I take them. They don't know I stopped a week ago and am starting to feel like myself again, that I'm starting to feel. Maybe I needed them when I came home from school, maybe I would have lost my mind without them, but I don't need them anymore.

If I could just get into the safe, I know I'd find the proof I need. All the dirty secrets are locked up in the safe.

"The poor girl," Paige said.

"The safe was open the night of the murder," I told her.

14 August

It's going to be tonight.

Vernita came to tell me Jerry's mother was on the phone. She called to see how I was doing. We talked for a while, we cried together, and she told me I needed to get on with my life, that he would have wanted me to. She's right, I know that, and maybe I'd be better now if I'd stopped taking the pills sooner. After I talked to her, Vernita came back to my room to check on me. Mother and Gram were out. They'd fire Vernita if they knew she let me talk to Mrs. Perrilloux.

Vernita is the only ally I have in this house. She

*loved Jerry as much as I did, maybe more. She is the
only one who really understands.*

*I am going to talk to Dad tonight. I'm going to find
out the truth.*

And the truth shall set me free.

"That was the day Wendell was shot," Paige said.
"Alais was going to confront her father about Jerrell."

My heart ached for Alais, but something niggled at
the back of my mind.

My cell phone rang.

"Yes, Abby?"

"Chanse, I found her. You'll never believe what she
told me."

CHAPTER ELEVEN

I ARRIVED AT JEPH and Abby's a little after eight on Saturday morning. The trip to the Irish Channel was uneventful, and I was wondering if maybe the Feds were right about Vinnie flying the coop. But I remained wary. I'd wanted to jump in my car the moment Abby called me, but Abby had begged off. She'd traced Alais to the Monteleone Hotel in the French Quarter and was taking her back to the shotgun house on Constantinople Street she shared with Jeph. Abby had not only found Alais, she'd managed to earn her trust. (I was definitely going to have to give her a raise.) Since then the mayor had ordered mandatory evacuation. Ginevra had strengthened to Category 5, and was predicted to make landfall late Sunday evening. There was still time for me to talk to Alais.

Abby introduced me to Alais and went to get coffee in the kitchen. Jephtha was undoubtedly asleep in their bedroom at the back of the house, not being an early riser.

Alais glared at me. "I'm over eighteen and I have my

own money," she said defiantly. "You can't make me go back."

She was definitely Cordelia Sheehan's grandchild.

Alais was much prettier in person than she'd seemed in her myspace photo. Her thick, dark red ponytail with golden highlights reached halfway down her back. Her eyes were so dark they were almost black. Like her grandmother, her face was heart-shaped, with prominent cheekbones, a pert nose and the full red lips most women get from a dermatologist's needle. Her skin was pale with a hint of gold, with a few freckles scattered across her nose and cheeks. A red Ole Miss T-shirt with blue script and low-rise jeans shorts complemented her short, petite frame, as did the pale pink toenail polish visible on her shoeless feet.

We were sitting in Abby and Jeph's living room, Alais on the dilapidated sofa and I in an uncomfortable reclining chair with broken springs that should have gone to the garbage men years ago. Jeph's aged golden retrievers, Greta and Rhett, had curled up on either side of Alais. Greta was sleeping, but Rhett kept shoving his head under Alais's hand whenever she stopped stroking him. His thumping tail drummed a steady tattoo on the sofa cushions.

The room itself was dim and somber. The dingy beige walls were bare. Abby and Jeph had nailed the shutters closed against the coming storm. Some morning light broke through the slats, but it was a losing battle against the dark. Several of the light bulbs on the ceiling fan/chandelier had burned out, and the slowly rotating fan blades seemed just to stir up more dust. Magazines and newspapers were scattered on the coffee table and the bare hardwood floor. The DVD player underneath the television was blinking 12:00. Abby tried her best to keep the house neat, but dog hair and the relentless New Orleans dust were winning the fight.

"Actually, I was hoping you could clear up some things for me," I told Alais, trying not to sound patronizing. "Are you willing to do that?"

Abby returned with three steaming mugs, each of which had a Disney villainess on it. I got Ursula the Sea Witch. The coffee was exactly the way I liked it—with a packet of sweetener and cream.

"Remember, Chanse is on *your* side," Abby said softly as she handed Alais a mug. "We both are."

She shooed Rhett off the couch and sat beside Alais, curling her legs underneath her. She was wearing a Catbox Club T-shirt and a pair of jeans shorts. Her feet were bare and her hair was tied back. She'd kept Cruella de Vil for herself.

Alais took a big drink from Maleficent. "Gram's paying him, isn't she?" she responded to Abby.

"And *he's* paying *me*," Abby pointed out. "If we intended to take you home, we would have called your family last night. We want what's best for you, Alais."

"That's what Gram and Mom always tell me. Don't I have any say in it? I'm not a child, and I'm tired of being treated like one."

"Tell Chanse everything, Alais, and we'll help you however we can."

She nodded in my direction. I picked up the cue.

"Why did you run away, Alais?" I asked as sympathetically as possible.

"I didn't run away. I wanted to get out of that house, to get my head together. I'm tired of being treated like I'm crazy."

With her jaw set, Alais's resemblance to Cordelia was both eerie and unsettling.

"I don't think you are, Alais. I know what it's like to lose someone you love."

Her eyes filled. "Do you ever get over it?"

I thought about lying, but decided she deserved honesty. She got enough lies at home.

"No, you never do. You learn to live with it, and eventually you get to the point where you don't think about it every day."

It had taken me about two years, but there was no need to tell her that.

"I'm so sick of that *time heals* bullshit. Is that supposed to make me feel better somehow? Being drugged out of your mind doesn't help much either. And the worst of it is . . ."

"Start at the beginning, Alais," Abby encouraged. "It's okay, you can trust Chanse."

She wiped her eyes. "I've loved Jerrell ever since I was a little girl," she said. "He was always a sweet boy, and fun—he always made me laugh."

"How did you meet him? Did you go to school with him?" I asked. I knew she hadn't, but it was a good way to get her talking.

"He was always around. Our housekeeper is his great-aunt. She never had any kids of her own, and she raised his mother. Jerrell's real grandparents died when his mom was a little girl. He called Vernita Grandma. She'd bring him to the house with her whenever she couldn't get a sitter. He was supposed to stay in the kitchen, but my real mom let him play with me, go swimming in the pool. And when she died . . . After that, Vernita never brought him around anymore. I missed him."

"Why did Vernita stop bringing Jerrell around?" I asked.

"I don't know. But he was my *friend*. That changed when we were in high school. He was at Ben Franklin. Gram wouldn't hear of me going to a public school, even if it was a magnet. I was trapped at Newman. I'm not sure exactly when our feelings changed from just being friends, but we kept it a secret."

"Because Jerrell was black?"

She looked at me like I was an idiot.

"Because his great-aunt was our *housekeeper*. The kids at Newman would have *loved* that. And Gram would never have allowed it. I was afraid they'd fire Vernita. And they would have, too. He got a full scholarship to Ole Miss—that was why I decided to go there. Gram wanted me at Vanderbilt, but I never mailed the application. She was pissed. I stood up to her, and Dad and Mom both took my side."

"Was that unusual?"

"It wasn't like Dad was really on my side. He never cared about me or noticed anything I did." She stated this as a matter of fact, absent of bitterness or sadness. "He just liked to piss off Gram. Janna said she thought I should go to school wherever I wanted to, it was my life, and Gram needed to get used to the idea I could make my own decisions. Gram was so mad, but there wasn't anything she could do about it."

"Did you like your stepmother? Did the two of you get along?"

"I was scared of her at first—you know, that whole 'wicked stepmother' thing—but she was great. She said I didn't have to call her Mom if I didn't want to, it was my decision. I called her Janna at first, and then I started calling her Mom. Whenever I needed anything, she was there for me. She never missed anything at school, you know, when I was in plays or stuff. Dad never came, Gram did sometimes, but Janna was always there. She was my friend. I could count on her. This summer, though, she's been different. Distant, like she had something on her mind."

Maybe like being raped and abused by your father. According to Janna, the rape happened four months ago, in May. That put it just before Jerrell's murder.

"Tell me about Jerrell, Alais," I said gently. "What happened to him?"

"Jerrell was—" Her voice broke. "He was the nicest guy, not like the other ones. He respected me, didn't push me. And he was smart, too. Pre-med. He wanted to work for Doctors Without Borders, go to Africa and help out. It was all Carey's fault. He didn't mean to, I know that, but not meaning to do something isn't much different from meaning to, if the result is the same. He came up to visit me at school. He always knew about Jerrell and me, I never kept it a secret from him. He used to help me sometimes—you know, when I needed to sneak out of the house to see Jerrell. He'd cover for me. It was our little secret. We had so much fun when he came up that weekend. But he took pictures of us and Janna found them, and the next weekend *she* came to see me, to talk to me about Jerrell. She told me to break it off, that Dad and Gram would never let me marry him. I told her I loved him, and they could just deal with it. I made up my mind that when I came home I would tell them, and if they didn't like it, well, too damned bad. Somehow Dad found out. I didn't want to think Janna told him, because she'd said she wouldn't, but how else would he know?"

"What happened when he found out?"

"It was horrible. He called me at school and screamed at me that I was a whore, that it was about time I started acting like a Sheehan."

"Did he threaten Jerrell?"

"He told me if I didn't break it off, *he* would take care of it and I wouldn't like his solution. I told him to go to hell. A weekend later, Jerrell was killed."

She broke down. Abby put her arm around her, and Alais buried her face in Abby's shoulder. Her body shook. The two of us sat quietly until she subsided.

"I'm sorry," she sniffled, sitting up again. "We'd gone out to dinner with some of our friends. Jerrell had a paper he had to finish, so he dropped me off at the Kappa house and went back to his apartment." Her lower lip trembled. "He had his own little studio. He worked at a coffee shop to pay the rent. He was supposed to meet me for coffee the next day, but he didn't show up and didn't answer his phone. I found him."

"You poor thing." I also knew what it was like to find the person you loved brutally killed. I couldn't imagine having to deal with it at nineteen. "But the news reports said his manager from the coffee shop found him."

"When he wasn't answering his phone, I went over there. The door was ajar. I saw him lying on the floor, in all that blood. I got out of there as fast as I could, went back to the Kappa house."

She wiped the tears away. Her eyes blazed.

"And I just *knew*." She spat the words out. "Dad was behind it. The police said it was a robbery—his wallet was gone, and his computer, and his DVD player. But his computer was ancient, and he never had any money. He didn't have *anything*. Then Gram came with her goddamn doctor. They shot me up with drugs and dragged me home. Janna—Mom—said she hadn't told Dad, but she must have been lying. How else would he have known? If I'd just done what he said, Jerrell would be alive."

"It isn't your fault, Alais," Abby said gently.

"You can't think that, Alais," I added. I knew saying it wouldn't help. Everyone had told me that, too. I hadn't believed it, either. "You don't have any proof?"

"If I'd had proof, I'd have gone to the police. I told that stupid cop up at Oxford, but he didn't believe me. The asshole acted like I was crazy. But it was him, I know it, I kept calling those stupid cops up there, to tell them, but they wouldn't listen. Gram took me to some psychiatrist. He didn't believe me, either, kept telling me I was delusional. He put me on pills. Gram kept track, to make sure I was taking them. Every night she'd come to my room and count them. I was a zombie all summer."

"Did they help at all?" I asked, although I knew the answer.

"When I was medicated it didn't hurt anymore, so the pills helped that way. I didn't feel anything when I was taking them. Two weeks ago, Vernita told me to stop, that I had to face the pain or it would never go away. So I stopped taking them. And once I could think clearly again, it all started making sense. Gram wanted me doped up so I'd forget that Dad killed Jerrell." She stifled a sob. "My own *grandmother* did that to me."

Abby hugged her again. "It's okay, Alais. Go ahead and cry, if you need to."

Alais pulled away.

"I can cry later."

She was Cordelia's granddaughter, all right.

She looked me right in the eyes.

"Gram still counted my pills every night. I flushed them down the toilet so she wouldn't know I wasn't taking them. I started listening to their conversations when they thought they were alone. As far as they knew I was drugged out. They weren't paying attention to me. One night I heard Gram and Dad arguing in the drawing room. She told him he was playing a very dangerous game, and she couldn't go on covering things up for him. He needed to get rid of everything in the safe, because if anyone ever found it, he'd go to jail and there wasn't anything she could do about it. He just laughed. He said he'd changed the combination, and wouldn't tell her the new one. I knew if I could just get into the safe, I'd be able to prove he killed Jerrell.

"I tried to get the combination. I went through his desk, went through everything, but I couldn't find it. On Monday, I decided to confront him."

"What happened?" I leaned forward.

"I heard him pull into the driveway. It was just after nine. I remember looking at the clock. It took me maybe ten, fifteen minutes to get up my nerve, then I left my room. He and Janna were in the drawing room, arguing. I went down the stairs and listened. She wanted a divorce. She said she wasn't going to raise another child in that house. He just laughed at her, told her he'd fight her, he'd take us kids away from her and make sure she never saw us. She told him to go ahead, when she was through with him he wouldn't be able to get elected dogcatcher. 'Who'd vote for a murderer?' she said. Janna *knew*. All along, she knew he'd killed Jerrell and never said anything.

"I couldn't listen anymore. I ran across the hall to the library and closed the door. My head was spinning, I could hardly breathe. I got the gun out of Gram's desk and loaded it. I don't know how long I sat there, trying to work up my nerve. I didn't want to kill him. I was just going to use the gun to scare him, to make him open the safe and tell me the truth. I had to do it—for Jerrell. And then I heard the shot."

"You never left the library?"

"Not until I heard the shot. I dropped Gram's gun into the drawer and ran across the hall. Dad was on the floor. There was blood everywhere. I saw the gun. I picked it up and screamed.

"And then Janna was there. *Alais, what have you done?* she shouted. Gram took the gun and wiped it with her shirt. She told Janna to get me out of there. I was hysterical. We were on the stairs when I heard another shot. Janna got me to my room, made me take a pill, told me that if anyone ever asked, I'd never left it, had my headphones on, didn't hear anything. That's what I told the police."

"You didn't see or hear anyone else with your father before the shot?"

She shook her head vehemently.

"After the shot?"

"I didn't kill my father. You have to believe me." She laughed bitterly. "But why would you? My own *family* doesn't. I tried telling them, but Gram and Janna refused to believe me."

"That's why she left," Abby said.

"I believe you, Alais," I said.

"You do?" She seemed startled.

The pieces were starting to fit together in my head. It all made sense now. The nonsensical story Janna and Cordelia had been trying to pass off as true—they'd been trying to protect Alais. But the only thing they'd succeeded in doing was letting the real killer get away with it.

"Yes, Alais, I do. But you've left something out, haven't you? You know who killed your father."

She shrank back against the couch.

"Alais," I coaxed. "You were in the library a long time, almost an hour and a half. While you were in there, you could hear your parents arguing, right?"

She nodded.

"You said as soon as you heard the shot, you ran across the hall. Unless the killer moved at superhuman speed, there is no way you couldn't have seen who it was."

I gave her a smile.

"You can tell us, Alais. It's okay," Abby encouraged.

"I don't know! Why won't you believe me?"

"Who was it, Alais?" I said.

I'd miscalculated. She froze up, and refused to say anything further. Either she really didn't know or wasn't going to tell us. But I was pretty sure I knew anyway.

My cell phone rang. I didn't recognize the number. I debated not answering it, but thought it might be the U.S. Marshals with an update on Vinnie.

"MacLeod."

"This is Meredith Cole," a ragged voice whispered. "From the Allegra Gallery? I talked to you last night? I need your help. Can you come to the gallery?"

"I'm sorry, Ms. Cole. I'm kind of busy right now. Can this wait?"

"Please! Kenny's dead!" she screamed into the phone. "And the police won't come!"

"I'm on my way."

I knelt in front of Alais and took her hands in mine.

"Alais, will you answer a different question?"

She looked miserable.

"What happened the night your mother died?"

"How would I know?" she responded, clearly surprised. "Gram and I were in Paris."

It all made sense now.

"I have to go out for a little while. But when I'm done, I'm coming back here and taking you home, Alais."

"No."

"There's a hurricane heading for the city," I said calmly. "Your family is worried about you, and you can't stay here."

Abby followed me onto the porch.

"I don't know how long I'll be, but I'm counting on you to convince her, Abby."

"I don't know if I can talk her into it, Chanse. She seems pretty determined not to go back there. I can't say that I blame her."

"Me, either." I said. "But promise me you'll work on her? I've got to run downtown."

"What's going on, Chanse?"

"I think I've figured it out. I'll tell you when I'm sure of it. In the meantime, Kenneth Musgrave is dead, and I need to get over to the gallery. From there I'll go to the Sheehan house. Then I'll call you. Don't tell Alais, okay?"

She nodded. I kissed her cheek.

"Good work, Abby. After the hurricane we'll talk about that raise."

"If you think I'll forget because of the storm, you're wrong!" she called after me.

When I tried to reach Venus, a mechanical voice informed me that all circuits were busy and to try again later. Irritated, I threw the phone into my passenger seat and turned on the radio as I got into the line of cars on Magazine heading toward the highway.

The latest projections showed New Orleans directly in the path of Ginevra. The storm surge coming into Lake Pontchartrain could reach thirty feet. The governor had requested aid from the Federal government, and National Guard units were mobilizing throughout the Southern states. The low-lying coastal parishes were already ordered to evacuate, and the order for Orleans Parish would come at noon. Anyone who remained in the city would be on their own until conditions were considered safe for first responders to get into the affected areas. That meant *after* the storm had passed. State buses were lining up at the Superdome and other sites throughout the metropolitan area for those without transportation out of New Orleans, with a limit of one suitcase per passenger. A toll-free number was provided for anyone who needed a lift to the staging areas. Pets would be transported by the Louisiana SPCA. No hotel rooms were available on I-10 West before Houston. The Red Cross was setting up the Cajundome in Lafayette as a shelter, but only for people bused in from New Orleans. Traffic reports estimated a thirteen-hour drive to the Texas state line. I-10 East was closed off. Contraflow lanes on I-10 West would open at noon. The mayor urged everyone to leave as soon as possible.

I turned off the radio. What had the Katrina surge been? Twenty-five feet? More than enough to crumble levees and destroy most of the city. Who would come back this time? Who would want to?

My entire body shook. My eyes filled with water. I told myself to get a grip, I had work to do.

Other than the cars crawling along Magazine Street, the city was like a ghost town. All the businesses along the street were boarded up. A sign at the gas station at the corner at Washington read *Go away you bitch!* Plastic bags covered the pump handles. My gas gauge still showed past full. Hopefully that would be enough to get me to Houston.

I turned left onto Washington to get out of the line of slow-moving cars, gambling there wouldn't be heavy traffic on Prytania, which didn't have an outlet to the highway. The gamble paid off. I flew up Prytania Street, turned left again at Felicity to get to St. Charles, and was forced to make a U-turn back to Prytania. I parked in front of Paige's house. The gallery wasn't far, and I'd get there faster on foot. I texted Venus to meet me, having once again gotten the damned circuits-busy message.

My heart was pounding. I started jogging, to burn off adrenaline. Calliope Street, the feeder road for the highway, was like a parking lot jammed with cars packed full of belongings, pets, and children. I weaved my way through them, focusing on the tall monument at Lee Circle, avoiding eye contact with passengers. Just as I got across I spotted a little black girl about seven years old, her hair twisted into three or four braids ending in beads sticking out from her scalp, a look of terror on her face. I gave her what I prayed was a reassuring smile, then looked down and moved faster.

Meredith Cole was sitting on the hood of the only car on Julia Street, a silver Honda Accord parked in front of the Allegra Gallery, smoking a cigarette. She flicked it into the street when she saw me. She was wearing flip-flops, a yellow LSU T-shirt, and purple LSU sweatpants.

"Thank you for coming," she said. "I didn't know who else to call."

"Tell me what happened," I responded, hoping that concentrating on work would calm my jangled emotions.

"I was getting ready to leave this morning. I'm going to my sister's in Baton Rouge." Her voice shook a bit. "I realized I'd left my wallet on my desk last night, I was in such a rush to get home. When I got here and put my key in the gallery door, it was already unlocked. I knew immediately something was wrong. I didn't want to go inside. I tried to call the police, but the circuits were busy. I needed to leave, and I needed my WALLET!"

She screamed the last few words and began sobbing hysterically.

Hating myself, I slapped her.

She gaped at me. Her knees buckled and I caught her, pushing her gently backward until she bumped against the car. I heaved her up until she was sitting on the hood.

"You *hit* me," she accused.

"I'm sorry," I said. "Are you okay now?"

"I'm all right."

"Please finish your story."

"I went inside. There was all this blood. Kenny was lying on the floor in the middle of it."

My phone buzzed. I pressed the message button and read Venus's text.

"The police are on their way," I said softly. "You've had a shock. Stay here and get hold of yourself while I look inside."

I left her sitting on the car.

All the gallery lights were on. I took my shirt off, wrapped it around my hands, pushed the door open, and carefully stepped inside. There were no footprints anywhere, nothing I could disturb.

Musgrave was wearing the same clothes he'd been wearing when I saw him yesterday. His shirt was covered in blood and had two bullet holes in it. His mouth was open. His lifeless eyes stared widely at the ceiling, a look of shock on his face. He hadn't been expecting death. The pool of blood was drying. He'd been dead a while.

I didn't waste sympathy on him. He was a murderer, even if I couldn't prove it at the moment.

I took pictures of everything with my phone, then went outside to wait for Venus.

CHAPTER TWELVE

THE GATES TO THE Sheehan mansion were open when I parked beside the silver Mercedes Vernita was loading with suitcases. The backseat of the black BMW next to it was packed to the roof. I parked and got out of my car.

"Evacuating?" I asked.

Vernita nodded. "Did you find Miss Alais?" She didn't look up from what she was doing.

"I've talked to her," I said.

"Well, that's for the best then. 'Bout time the truth came out."

"Is Miss Janna here?"

"She's in the library with Miss Cordelia. She drove down from Baton Rouge this morning."

"Thanks, Vernita. I'm truly sorry about Jerrell."

"Thank you."

The front door was ajar, so I let myself in. The door to the drawing room was closed. In the library, I could see Janna in the wingback chair. I rapped my knuckles on the door a couple of times to announce my presence. No response.

"We need to talk," I said, and walked into the room.

Janna Sheehan looked like she hadn't slept in days. Her hair was carelessly tied back, and she'd made no effort to conceal the dark smudges under her eyes with makeup. Her worn-looking gray fleece sweats had a hole at the right knee. Her feet were bare. She sat in the wingback chair with her legs curled beneath her, staring into her sweating glass of iced tea as though it could show her the future if she stared hard enough.

Even grande dame Cordelia seemed worse for wear, sitting at the desk with a glass of straight Scotch in her right hand. I wouldn't have been surprised to learn she'd put on her makeup without a mirror. Wisps of her usually immaculate hair rebelled against her hairspray. She wore a dove gray skirt and jacket over a white silk blouse, but no jewelry and no gloves. Her right calf had a run in the stockings.

I almost felt sorry for her.

Almost.

"Have you found Alais?" she asked.

Ignoring the question, I sat down and confronted them with the holes in their stories.

"I told you it wouldn't work, Cordelia," Janna said. "You're not as good at this as you used to be."

"Shut up, Janna," Cordelia snapped. She sounded defeated.

Janna's response caught me off guard. "What really

happened that night?" I asked her. "The truth, please. It's time for the lies to stop."

"Keep quiet, Janna!" Cordelia warned.

"It's no good, Cordelia. We should have just told the truth from the beginning. Alais wasn't in her right mind. That was the way we should have gone with it, scandal or no scandal. It's always better to tell the truth."

"What do you know about the truth?" Cordelia sneered. "You've told so many lies you can't even keep them straight anymore. Since you're such a fan of the truth, why don't you tell him who Carey's father is?"

Janna flushed. "It isn't relevant."

"Isn't it?" Cordelia sipped her Scotch.

"Actually, it isn't," I interjected. "I don't care who Carey's father is."

Janna smiled, inclining her head to me in a slight, almost mocking bow.

"Thank you, Mr. MacLeod."

She looked at her mother-in-law.

"The jig's up, Cordelia."

"What did you and Wendell argue about that night?" I asked. "And before you lie to me again, I know Wendell got home shortly after nine, not at eleven-thirty."

"They argued about her baby, isn't that right?" Cordelia hissed. "He knew it wasn't his, and he told her he was going to get a divorce and take the children away."

Janna leaped to her feet, knocking her iced tea off the side table. A puddle spread on the floor in the shattered glass. She was breathing hard.

"That's not true, you stupid, miserable old woman!"

"People thought I hated her because she wasn't good enough for Wendell," Cordelia went on, red spots appearing on her cheeks. "I didn't care that her father was a janitor. What I cared about was my son marrying a slut without the morals of a common alley cat. Isn't that what happened that night, Janna? When you told him you were pregnant, didn't he tell you he wasn't going to pass your little bastard off as his own? Isn't that why you killed him?"

A slow smile spread across Janna's face as she sat down again in her chair.

"I take it back, Cordelia. You're still very good at this kind of thing. But I didn't kill Wendell—and he knows." She turned to me. "You found Alais, didn't you? And she's talked?"

I nodded, playing along.

"Game over, Cordelia."

Her mouth worked slightly, but she said nothing. Then her shoulders sagged and she crumpled in her chair. Her hands came to her face, and for just a moment her shoulders shook. When she took her hands away, she was no longer Cordelia Spencer Sheehan, head of one of the most powerful families in Louisiana, but just a sad old woman broken under her burdens. It was horrible to watch, but I couldn't look away.

"She can't go to jail," she said, her voice quavering. "She wasn't in her right mind. She hasn't been all summer."

Janna got up from her chair, sat down next to Cordelia and put her arms around her. Cordelia lowered her head onto Janna's shoulder. Janna stroked her hair.

I found it hard to believe what I was seeing. I couldn't stop staring at the two women.

Janna looked at me. "What's next?" she said.

"What really happened that night, Janna?" I asked.

"Wendell got home around nine," she said. Her voice was strong and authoritative. "I was in the drawing room. He'd been drinking."

"You were waiting for him, weren't you? And you had the gun."

"I didn't take the gun. I was going to leave him. I was going to get a divorce. You see the damage he did to Alais and Carey. I wasn't about to let him do that to another child." She looked at Cordelia. "He laughed at me, told me if I left, he'd see to it that I never saw the children again. But I had an ace of my own to play."

"You knew he'd been behind Jerrell's death," I said. "And you threatened to expose him."

"It was a bluff. I didn't have any proof. But it worked. It scared the crap out of him. I told him I'd also charge him with raping me, with physically abusing me, spraining my wrist. I told him if he didn't let me and the children go, not only would he never get elected to public office again, he'd go to jail."

Another piece clicked into place. I returned her smile.

"You're still lying, Janna."

"I don't know what you mean."

"You didn't just suspect he'd had Jerrell Perrilloux killed. You had a private eye of your own. He volunteered in the campaign office." I grasped for the name Rory Delesdernier had given me. "Dave Zeringue."

"That's not his real name," Janna said. "But yes, he got the evidence for me."

"And you gave Wendell copies of it. Copies of checks going back ten years, made out to Kenny Musgrave."

She looked genuinely confused. "I don't know anything about that."

Cordelia raised her head wearily, also confused.

"Jerrell Perrilloux? What does Vernita's nephew have to do with anything? Why would Wendell have him killed?"

"Who knows why Wendell did anything?" Janna replied bitterly. "I just assumed it was because he was black."

I looked at Cordelia. "You didn't know Alais was involved with him?"

Cordelia's face went white. "I didn't know—about Alais, or his murder."

Janna patted her hand again.

"I knew that, Cordelia. If you'd had anything to do with it, it wouldn't have been so easy to get the evidence. There would have been no evidence to find."

She got up for a glass of water.

"Wendell didn't pull the trigger himself," she explained. "He was at least that smart. He used his usual fixer."

"Kenny Musgrave," I said.

"He sent Kenny to Oxford to kill that boy. My detective found the gun, he traced the money transfer, everything. He gave me all the evidence that afternoon. It was my leverage. Wendell argued, but he agreed to my demands. It was either that or jail. I left him in the drawing room, went upstairs to my room, and locked the door. That's when I noticed my gun was missing. I wanted to have it ready, in case he got even drunker. I didn't trust him. I wasn't going to wind up at the bottom of the stairs with my neck broken, like Grace did."

"Why didn't you tell me?" Cordelia said hoarsely.

"I should have," Janna said. "I didn't know . . . Alais must have overheard us arguing."

"She heard everything," I confirmed.

"That poor, poor girl," Janna responded. "It must have been a shock. No wonder she did what she did."

I ignored this. "What happened next?"

"I stayed in my room until I heard the gunshot. I went downstairs and saw Alais standing with the gun in her hands. I may have said something. I don't remember. I was so shocked I wasn't thinking clearly. I don't know how long I stood there."

"I heard the shot and knew something horrible had happened." Cordelia's voice shook. "I didn't know what Janna was planning. I ran down the stairs and saw them both standing there, and I knew I had to take charge. Alais was about to fall to pieces and Janna was in shock. I took the gun away from Alais and told Janna to get her upstairs. I wiped the gun free of prints and checked to see if Wendell had a pulse. He didn't. I fired the gun into the floor."

"When I came back down, Cordelia told me what to say when the police arrived," Janna continued the narrative. "I told her I didn't think the two of us accusing each other would work, that she was crazy for firing the gun."

With an effort of will, Cordelia straightened herself into her familiar rigid posture.

"Like I was going to allow *you* to implicate yourself? Risk having you tried while carrying my grandson?"

"Alais didn't kill her father," I told them.

Their heads swiveled to me in shock.

"What?" Cordelia said.

"But we *saw* her."

"You didn't see her pull the trigger."

I turned to Cordelia. "Did it never occur to you that the story you concocted—that you walked in, saw Wendell lying there, and picked up the gun—is exactly what Alais did?"

Neither woman answered me.

"What was in the safe?" I asked.

"I have no idea," Janna replied. "I never had access to it."

"Cordelia?" I said.

She shook her head.

"Wendell changed the combination several months ago. Before that? Stocks, money, some papers. Nothing out of the ordinary. I just assumed Wendell had opened it that night before Alais shot him. I inventoried the contents for the police, since the safe was open. As far as I could tell, nothing was missing. And since the jewelry and money were still there . . ."

"Alais didn't shoot Wendell," I said. "Someone else was in the house that night. After Janna left him, they forced Wendell to open the safe, then shot him. Does either of you recognize these?"

I opened my bag and tossed the photocopied checks on the table. Janna shook her head and passed them to Cordelia.

"Kenny Musgrave." She spat out the words.

"Kenny Musgrave claimed that Alais saw Wendell kill Grace. According to Kenny, that was why Wendell released Grace's trust and wrote these checks every month after she died. Musgrave was a liar. Alais wasn't even here the night her mother died. Care to clear that up, Cordelia?"

Cordelia's face was a mask.

"We were in Europe when Grace died. I always thought it was a tragic accident."

"You never once thought about how similar Grace's death was to Roger Palmer's? It never occurred to you that one murder served as the blueprint for the other? I find that hard to believe. Grace was planning to leave Wendell. She saw a divorce lawyer that very afternoon. She was going to take Alais with her. But she made one major mistake. She told her brother what she was going to do."

Cordelia's expression never changed.

"Kenny was always looking for a leg up," I went on.

"I suspect he'd done Wendell's dirty work for him before. I don't know if we'll ever know exactly what happened—whether Wendell ordered Kenny to kill Grace or if Kenny did it on his own initiative. Whatever the truth is, Kenny got his timing wrong. Wendell would never have used his mistress as an alibi for Grace's death. I also don't understand why Wendell thought Grace had to die. A divorce wouldn't have hurt his career. Politicians nowadays get divorced all the time, and still get elected."

"I suspected something." Cordelia said finally. "But I didn't want to know."

"How many of Wendell's murders did you cover up for him? Or just look away from?" I asked casually. I was enjoying watching the old woman squirm. "I know about three of them. How many more were there?"

"I don't know what you're talking about."

I ticked them off on my fingers. "The first was Roger Palmer. Then your daughter-in-law, Grace. Then Jerrell Perrilloux. Alais thinks Jerrell was killed because he was related to your housekeeper. I don't buy that. I think it was because he was black, and Wendell didn't like the idea of mixed-race grandkids any more than you did."

Cordelia glared at me, her posture remaining rigid.

"Grace, too?" Janna said, bewildered. "I guess I *was* lucky Monday night." She gave Cordelia a malicious smile. "Answer him, Cordelia. I'd like to know myself."

Cordelia poured herself a Scotch from the decanter on a sideboard, then raised her glass to the portrait of her husband on the wall, took a drink, and turned to the two of us.

"Roger Palmer was an accident. It wasn't my idea to cover it up. Bobby was afraid of the scandal. When Wendell called that night . . . Sure, there would have been a scandal and it might have hurt Bobby's administration, but I thought covering it up was a mistake. The truth has a way of coming out."

She sat down across from me.

"He was my only child, Mr. MacLeod. I don't expect you to understand."

"What's to understand? You made yourself an accessory after the fact. I doubt any jury would convict you. I doubt you'd even be prosecuted. It's amazing how the rich and powerful can get away with murder."

"Roger Palmer was an accident," she insisted.

"Grace wasn't an accident," I countered. "Why else would Wendell release the trust she left for Musgrave? Why would Wendell have paid him over half a million dollars in ten years, if not as payment for murder?"

"I'd like to know that myself," Janna said.

Cordelia emptied the Scotch. "I had my suspicions, of course. It was almost an exact reenactment of the story we came up with for Roger. But Wendell always insisted it *had* happened that way—that she tripped on the stairs. And Grace left no trust for Kenny Musgrave."

"I guess we'll never know for sure," I said. "Wendell certainly felt the need to pay him off. Given that Wendell paid Musgrave to kill Jerrell—"

Cordelia interrupted me. "Why did Wendell have

that boy killed? Because he was involved with Alais? I don't believe it. We weren't racists. Having his daughter involved with a black boy might have lost him the racist vote, but—"

I raised my hand to stop her.

The funny thing about rich people is that, no matter how liberal they may be in their hearts, the people who work for them only exist when they choose to notice them—especially the people who work in their homes. I'd heard the front door open, heard footsteps in the hall, heard them stop. She'd been out there listening for a good ten to fifteen minutes.

"Vernita? Will you come in here?"

She entered the library with her head held high.

"What does Vernita have to do with any of this?" Cordelia demanded.

I had a theory about that.

"What was the *real* problem, Vernita?" I asked gently. "Why did Wendell have such a problem with Jerrell and Alais dating that he had the boy killed?"

"Because they were brother and sister," she said defiantly.

The last piece of the puzzle fell into place.

The next few moments were chaotic. Cordelia crumpled to the floor. Janna exclaimed and rushed to her side, massaging Cordelia's wrists and talking to her in a gentle murmur.

Vernita gave me a sad little smile. She was beautiful, I realized, and not much younger than Cordelia. Her shoulders were bowed and her hands red and cracked from a lifetime of hard work, yet she held herself with dignity. She was slight, her skin dark, her graying hair pulled back into a tight bun.

It hadn't been about class, as I'd believed. I remembered looking at Jerrell's picture and thinking he looked familiar.

I was vaguely aware of Cordelia sitting up with Janna's help, Janna getting her a glass of water, then helping her to her feet and into a chair.

"Are you okay?" I asked, not taking my eyes from Vernita.

"Fine," Cordelia croaked. "Vernita, I know I didn't hear you right."

Vernita turned her head slowly to look at her long-time employer.

"Yes, ma'am, you heard me right. Mr. Wendell was Jerrell's daddy."

"But how— How is that possible?"

Cordelia was struggling to regain her composure.

"He had sex with my niece, ma'am. More than once. Don't you remember? Dinah worked here that summer I wasn't well. She came around to help out. Mr. Wendell was engaged to Miss Grace then. If I'd had any idea what was going on, I woulda put a stop to it. I didn't know till she got pregnant."

"Why didn't you tell me?"

Cordelia's face was pale. The glass of water shook in her hand.

"So you could do what? Buy her off, make her give her baby away?"

Vernita didn't even try to mask her contempt.

"Oh no, Mr. Wendell couldn't keep his pants on, but I worked here long enough by then to know what the deal woulda been. You'da said she was just some gold-diggin' tramp after money. It would all be her fault."

She turned to me.

"Dinah was a stupid girl. She thought Mr. Wendell would marry her. I tol' her she might as well just slit her own throat if she tol' him. I used to bring the boy around just to see if any of you folks *noticed* how much he looked like his daddy. But none of you did. To you he was just another nigger boy.

"Then Jerrell got sick," Vernita went on, "and she didn't have no insurance. So Dinah tol' Miss Grace. I was so mad at that girl. I tol' her no good would come of it. Miss Grace gave her the money, all right, and the next day she died. I tol' Dinah, 'That could happen to you if you don't keep your damn fool mouth shut.' I don't know if Miss Grace tol' Mr. Wendell or not. I don't think she did, cuz Mr. Wendell wouldn'ta let it rest."

"And then Jerrell started seeing Alais," I said.

"I thought they was just friends." Her voice shook for the first time. "Jerrell didn't tell me the truth. If he did, I woulda tol' him. When I saw those pictures Mr. Carey took . . . I knew I had to stop them afore it went too far."

Tears streamed from her eyes, but her body remained still.

"I didn't know what to do. So I got his birth certificate and showed it to Mr. Wendell. I tol' him we had to stop them afore they did somethin' against God. Mr. Wendell, he thank me. He tol' me he'd go talk to Jerrell. But he kept the birth certificate. He put it in the safe. And then Jerrell got killed." Her shoulders shook. "I thought Mr. Wendell— But he was here all that weekend. He even put up a reward."

"But you still suspected him, didn't you?"

"Well, Miss Grace died after she found out, didn't she? But I wasn't sure. I went down to the hospital to get a copy of the birth certificate . . . and it was gone. No one had it anywhere. The only thing to prove my Jerrell was Mr. Wendell's son was locked up in that safe. That convinced me Mr. Wendell had my boy killed. He didn't want no one to know. That Monday I decide I gonna get the birth certificate back. I take Miss Janna's gun. I come back to the house and let myself in through the kitchen like I always do. I leave my car out on the street. I heard him and Miss Janna fightin' in the drawing room. I heard what she said about him having that Musgrave man do his dirty work—killing my Jerrell— for him. I wait until she go back upstairs. I walk in the drawing room and point the gun at him. I tol' him I want Jerrell's birth certificate and I'd kill him just as soon as look at him. He open the safe, and then come back at me. He say I'd never shoot him." Her jaw set. "I pull the trigger. When he go down, I go to the safe. There was a folder with Jerrell's name on it. I take it and run out the front door. When I get home, all that was in the folder was the birth certificate and them canceled check copies. I put them through your mail slot."

"And last night you killed Kenny Musgrave."

"I wait until that tall woman leave, and then I knock on the door. He know who I am, so he let me in. I pulled out the gun and said, 'This for Jerrell'—and I shot him."

Except for Cordelia's labored breathing, the room was silent.

"What are you doing?" she asked as I took my phone from my pocket.

"Calling the police."

"You *can't*!"

Vernita smiled at me sadly. "You go right ahead, Mr. MacLeod. I'm ready to face judgment and make my peace."

"You can't," Cordelia insisted. "I'll pay you. Alais can never know the truth! Remember what happened when she just thought the boy died and her father was responsible? If she finds out he was her brother—what if they— You *can't*."

She looked pleadingly at me.

"I don't have to tell the police *why* I killed Mr. Wendell, do I, Mr. MacLeod?" Vernita asked.

I wavered for a moment. I've always believed the truth was more important than lies. I couldn't think of a better example than the Sheehan family. Maybe Roger Palmer's death *had* been an accident. But by covering up the truth, Cordelia had taught her son that when you have money and position and power, you can get away with murder. He'd learned the lesson well, and as a result, Grace and Jerrell were murdered when they became problems for him. Everything had come full circle with the deaths of Wendell and Kenny Musgrave. I understood why Vernita had killed them. It wasn't only because they'd killed her grandnephew. It was because she knew they'd never pay for their crimes. There would be no justice for her Jerrell.

The law took a dim view of vigilante justice, no matter how well deserved it was. No matter what her motivations, Vernita had broken the law and would have to pay for it. She had neither the money nor the connections to get away with it. A lawyer like Loren McKeithen could sway a jury with sympathy for an old woman of color who'd killed the white men who killed her grandnephew. The fact that Jerrell had been Wendell's son would only work in her favor. What kind of man hired someone to kill his own blood? And Kenny Musgrave was a despicable man as well. He'd killed his own sister for money. A black jury just might let Vernita off. Yet she was willing not only to confess to what she'd done, but to protect Alais by not telling the whole truth to the police.

It wasn't fair. The entire thing made me sick to my stomach. Just standing in the house made me feel corrupt.

"I'm not a lawyer, Vernita," I said finally. "But I'm calling the police."

"Please, Mr. MacLeod," Cordelia pleaded. "We have to protect Alais."

"With all due respect, Mrs. Sheehan, I feel badly for your granddaughter, but if I don't call the police I'm no better than you are. And I don't think I could live with myself knowing that."

As I walked out onto the porch and into the sunlight, I had no doubt that the moment I'd left the room Cordelia began hatching another scheme. I suppose I couldn't blame her. It was who she was, how she did things. I sat down on the steps and dialed Venus's cell phone.

Miracle of miracles, the call went through.

CHAPTER THIRTEEN

I FILLED VENUS AND Blaine in on everything, including Jerrell's parentage. Before they arrived, I wasn't sure I would. But I realized that Alais was stronger than either her stepmother or her grandmother had given her credit for. Her depression after Jerrell's murder had been normal. Instead of letting her deal with her grief, they'd put her in the care of some psychiatrist who thought the answer was to keep her in a drugged stupor. The Alais Sheehan I'd spoken to that morning was a survivor. Her world would be rocked when she learned the truth, especially if she'd slept with Jerrell, but I was certain she could handle it. In the future, Janna and Cordelia would have their hands full with that one.

I texted Abby that the police were at the Sheehans' and to bring Alais home, then waited for her response: *Roger, boss.* I got into my car hoping I'd heard the last of this family.

There was no traffic to be seen on the way back to Paige's, no signs of life anywhere, other than the occasional dive bar with its neon sign broadcasting OPEN as an enticement to whoever might have stayed behind to face down the storm that was less than twenty-four hours away. Even the side streets were empty. Apart from that, it could have been a normal summer day. The sun was shining, there were no clouds in the brilliant azure sky, and it was hotter than hell.

I switched on the radio. Ginevra had been downgraded to Category 3, but it looked as though New Orleans was going to take a direct hit, with the eye now projected to hit landfall at the mouth of Lake Borgne. I turned it off. Lake Borgne wasn't really a lake. It was a wide-mouthed bay. New Orleans East sat on a low-lying peninsula with Lake Borgne to the south and Lake Pontchartrain to the north. A narrow channel called the Rigolets connected the two brackish lakes. That was the path the destructive storm-surge from Katrina had followed—from the Gulf into Lake Borgne through the Rigolets into Lake Pontchartrain and into the canals penetrating the heart of the city. If that happened again, the levees would be overtopped and some would collapse. Once again, ninety percent of the city would be underwater. Those who hadn't evacuated would be trapped on roofs. Power and communications would shut down. Hopefully, the lessons learned from the last time would prevent a repeat of the horrible week that followed. But it looked like it could be the deathblow for New Orleans.

My hands shook. I pulled over to the curb, got out of my car, lit a cigarette, and drank in the beauty of the city.

The first time I'd come to New Orleans was also the night I fell in love with the city. It was like nothing I'd ever seen growing up in a small town forty-five minutes north of Houston. I was eighteen. I'd just begun college. As I walked the cracked and tilted sidewalks of the French Quarter, I knew this was where I belonged. Throughout my undergraduate years at LSU, I came down from Baton Rouge as often as I could, just waiting for the day I could move here for good. My two years on the police force had shown me the dark underside of the city: the crime, the poverty, the racism, the despair, and the broken system the Sheehan family epitomized. But despite all those problems, somehow the city was a joyous place that embraced everyone.

The Mardi Gras after Katrina had been amazing. A mere five months after the storm, the city had rallied and thrown a party to show the doubters and the haters of the world that New Orleans had survived and we would endure. I remembered walking up the parade route on Fat Tuesday, wearing a costume for the first time because it seemed like the right thing to do, and seeing the crowds cheering all along St. Charles. I remembered the signs—504EVER and ATLANTA THANKS AND LOVES YOU NEW ORLEANS and ST. BERNARD WE'LL BE BACK—and T-shirts saying things like *NOPD: Not Our Problem, Dude;* or *Campaign 2006: I'm for Cookie Monster;* or *FEMA: Fix Everything My Ass;* or *FEMA: Find Every Mexican Available;* or *I Stayed for Katrina and All I Got Was This Lousy T-shirt . . . and a flat-screen TV and a Cadillac and a stereo . . .* And the costumes! A group of women dressed as Brownies, only their sashes read *Heckuva Job*. A group of men dressed as UPS deliverymen sporting *What can Brown do for you?* on their backs. I saw incredibly flawless and over-the-top drag. It was almost too much to take in. Everyone was so happy and relaxed and having a good time laughing and dancing in the streets. What pride I'd felt in my city, and in my fellow New Orleanians! My eyes swam with tears of joy, my face ached from the huge grin I had on it all day. It was the first time since I'd evacuated that I truly believed New Orleans was going to come back, the first time it felt like *New Orleans* again. The magic hadn't gone away, it had just hibernated for a while.

I threw my cigarette in the gutter and got into my car. It would take a hell of a lot more than a goddamn act of nature to kill the spirit of New Orleans. We'd gotten through it before and we'd do it again if we had to, a thousand times over.

The only car parked on Polymnia was Paige's battered old Toyota. The backseat was piled high, but she'd left space for Nicky's carrier. Maybe the marshals were right about Vinnie having left town. I let myself in the gate and walked back to Paige's apartment. She was sitting on her steps, smoking a cigarette and crying. When she saw me, she wiped her face and forced a smile.

"So, how'd it go?"

I sat down beside her and put my arm around her.

"Case closed. It's in Venus and Blaine's hands now. Are you okay?"

"A little overwhelmed, I guess. Ginevra turned a bit, but it's worse than before."

"I heard it on the radio," I said.

"Not again, Chanse. It *can't* happen again."

"It might keep turning," I said, giving her a squeeze. "How many times before has that happened? Remember Ivan? And Jorges? Just keep thinking good thoughts."

There's something to be said for comforting another person. The more I talked, the more confidant I felt myself that Ginevra would keep turning west.

She put her head on my shoulder.

"I don't know if I can go through it all again, Chanse."

"We can handle it. And this time we know what to expect. The only thing I remember about getting out the last time was the shock and horror. It doesn't feel the same this time. Come on, let's go inside and watch some death-and-destruction television."

The Weather Channel showed a long line of cars on I-10 West, moving at a crawl out of the city. A pretty blonde woman with a serious expression told us the evacuation was going smoothly. There were some snarls in traffic exiting the city, but once the contraflow lanes were reached it went smoothly. Baton Rouge was now estimated at five to six hours away. The latest report from the National Hurricane Center showed Ginevra was still Category 3. Unfortunately, this had not lessened the projected storm surge it carried before it. Although the Army Corps of Engineers had stated that the levees damaged by Katrina had been repaired and could withstand a Category 3 storm surge, city residents were not reassured. All over the South, National Guard units had been called to duty. Relief supplies were being stockpiled and readied for transport.

Paige hit the mute button. "I think we should wait a few more hours before we hit the road," she said calmly, lighting a cigarette. "Let the traffic die down some more."

"It should lighten up by then," I agreed, not taking my eyes from the television.

"I could really use a drink," she added. "But . . ."

I didn't need to point out that it was a bad idea.

"I guess I should call my sister," I said. I'd been delaying all day, even though I knew she'd be worried about me.

"Use my landline. I'm going to start emptying out the refrigerator."

My sister picked up on the second ring. "Hey Daphne, it's Chanse," I said.

"Chanse!" Daphne half-shrieked. "I've been trying to call you all day! Please tell me you're on the road out of there!"

"I'll probably leave in a couple of hours."

"You're coming here," Daphne asserted. "I'll get the guest room ready and you can stay as long as you need to. I won't take no for an answer."

"Thanks, Daphne. How's Mom doing?"

"Better." She paused. "It meant a lot to her to see you. She's worried about this storm. I'll let her know you're staying here."

"Thanks. I'll call when I'm leaving. I'll send a text if I can't get through."

"Don't thank me," she said. "We're family."

"Talk to you soon."

Family.

Mothers.

When Daphne had called three weeks ago to tell me our mother had cancer and was dying, I hadn't wanted to go. I hadn't seen my family since the day I packed my car and left for LSU. I'd been so exhilarated when I passed the city limits sign heading south, as though I'd finally gotten out of prison. I was never going back to that trailer park on the bad side of town. I didn't care if I never saw my father again. He downed a six-pack of beer every night after getting home from the oil fields. His temper was uncertain and he wasn't afraid to use violence to vent it. And my mother, who never intervened when it happened. She always smelled of sour alcohol and didn't care how she looked. High school had been a misery until my talents on the football field made the other kids forget my worn-out Sears Roebuck clothing and my status as trailer trash. No, I was never going back, I swore as I took the on-ramp to I-10 and said goodbye to Cottonwood Wells and my family forever.

Daphne wrote to me at LSU, and I'd send her a card every now and then. As the years passed, I heard from her less and less. A card for my birthday, the wedding invitation, announcements about the birth of her kids, and of course Christmas. I never bothered to read the notes she wrote on the cards, just tossed them in the trash. I didn't care what was going on with my parents. I didn't want to know anything. I had a different life. I was a different person. No one in New Orleans knew I'd grown up in a trailer with a drunk for a mother and a violent father, and that was fine with me.

Paige and I had met for dinner at the Avenue Pub the night Daphne called. After a couple of drinks, I told Paige about it.

"Are you going?" she asked.

"No way," I said.

"I think you should."

"When was the last time you talked to *your* mother?" I snapped. "You cut your mother off just like I did."

"I'll never forgive my mother. Her boyfriend raped me and I had to get an abortion. I was thirteen, and she blamed me! You know that, Chanse. But if she were dying, I'd go see her. You *need* to do this."

So, I'd driven the six hours to Houston with a knot in my stomach and gone to see my mother at the M. D. Anderson medical facility, not knowing what to expect. The last time I'd been in a hospital had been the day Paul died. Would my father be there? My younger brother? What would I say to my mother after fifteen years?

I'd knocked on the open door to her room. The beautiful woman in a chair by the bed looked up and smiled at me.

"Chanse," my younger sister Daphne said, and ran across the room, throwing her arms around me and nearly knocking me down. She held on to me and sobbed. After a few awkward moments, I hugged her back. Finally, she pulled away from me.

"It's so good to see you," she whispered. "Go say hello."

I couldn't speak.

My mother was hooked up to tubes and monitors. Her eyes were closed. I cursed myself for not bringing flowers, or something. I stood there in silence, unsure of what I should do.

She'd lost weight, and aged. Her hair was shot through with gray around her wrinkled face, which was made up. (I found out later that Daphne did that for her every morning.) She looked like a shell of her former self.

Then her eyes opened, and her face softened. "Oh, Chanse," she said. Her eyes filled with tears and her chin trembled. "Thank you for coming. I'm so, so sorry."

In that instant, my life history was rewritten. I forgot the woman who always seemed to be complaining, who always smelled slightly of stale liquor as she chain-smoked her way through daily visits to the soap opera towns of Pine Valley, Llanview, and Port Charles. And I knew it wasn't the first time I'd done this.

The morning I left Cottonwood Wells, I'd been packing my car. My father was at work, Daphne was at her job, and my younger brother was off at baseball practice. I'd said perfunctory goodbyes to all of them and was coming back into the trailer to get another box of my stuff when my mother confronted me.

"I found this in your room," she said, her voice shaking and her eyes wild.

It was a *Playgirl* magazine I'd shoplifted from a bookstore in town about a year before. I'd forgotten all about it.

"It's not mine," I said automatically.

She slapped my face. "Don't lie to me!"

In all my eighteen years, my mother had never raised a hand to me. That was my father's job. She always used tears and guilt. I stood there and looked at her, not knowing what to say. Finally I responded.

"It's mine," I admitted petulantly.

She became hysterical, screaming at me about sin and God and how no son of hers was going to be a pervert. I'd never seen her so angry. I stood there under the barrage of words, getting angry myself, and more hurt by the second. All I could think was that I needed to get away, and that once I did I was never coming back.

When she finally stopped, her rage spent, she collapsed onto the couch and sobbed.

After a few moments, I said, "Goodbye, Mother," and walked out of the trailer for the last time. There were a few more boxes left, but I didn't care. All I wanted was to put as much distance between Cottonwood Wells and me as humanly possible.

I drove out of town with tears on my cheeks, forcing all my good memories of her out of my mind. I trained myself to remember only the bad. If I only remembered the bad stuff, it wouldn't hurt anymore.

As I stood by her hospital bed, I saw love and sorrow in her eyes, and I started remembering the good.

I remembered the woman who had walked me to my first day of school, the woman who'd gotten up at five every morning to make breakfast for my father before he left for work, and then made breakfast for the rest of us when we got up. I remembered the face that turned sad whenever we shopped for school clothes at the Sears in the mall instead of the Gap, the Levi's Store, and all the more chic places where the other kids' parents took them. The woman who packed my lunch every day with my favorite chips and sandwiches—and how much I resented not being able to buy lunch like the cool kids. I remembered the woman who came to every one of my football games, and when my name was called when they introduced the starters before the game, shouted louder than everyone else, loud enough that I knew it was her. I'd see her in the stands, jumping up and down and telling everyone around her, "That's my son! That's my SON!"

Finally, I remembered looking back in the rearview mirror as I fled the trailer park, and seeing her standing at the foot of the driveway when I sped off to LSU, her shoulders bent, crying as she waved goodbye to her son. She'd had a shock that rocked her world and didn't know how to deal with it, and had reacted badly. And she'd regretted that reaction every minute of every day ever since.

For the first time in years, looking down at my dying mother, I didn't see a monster. And God help me, I started crying as I stood there. She'd reached out and grabbed my hand.

"Shhh, baby, it's okay. All that matters is you're here now."

I sat down next to her bed, grateful for the chance I'd never had with Paul before he died.

"I love you, Mom," I managed to choke out.

The whole Sheehan case, really, had been about mothers and their children. Cordelia and Wendell. Janna and Carey, Grace and Alais, and of course, Vernita and Jerrell. Sure, Jerrell hadn't been Vernita's son, but she thought of him that way.

"Thanks again, Paige," I said.

"What are friends for?" she said quietly.

She turned up the sound on the television with the remote. The governor was holding a press conference, urging everyone who lived in the path of the storm to evacuate as soon as possible. He reiterated that there would be no rescues until after the storm had passed, when in any case the water supply would most likely be contaminated.

Paige muted him. "I hate that bastard."

"I don't like him either, but I have to give him credit," I said. "He's handling this crisis pretty well."

"It's easy when you've experienced the exact same crisis once already," Paige retorted. "They'll compare him favorably to Governor Blanco, who had, what? A whole three days to prepare? He called a state of emergency before the damned storm even entered the gulf."

"Maybe they've learned from the mistakes made last time."

"Whatever. I'm going to make a sandwich. You want anything?"

"Yeah." I wasn't hungry, but knew I needed to eat something.

We spent the next few hours talking, watching the clock as it slowly moved towards six. I wasn't looking forward to getting on the road. The traffic reports seemed to indicate some lessening on I-10—the drive to Baton Rouge was now projected to take a little more than four hours. Cameras showed the line of cars heading west. Ginevra was holding steady as a Category 3, and the slight turn to the west was continuing. The eye was projected to come ashore through Breton Sound, almost due south of Lake Borgne, by five-thirty. But the storm-surge was still going to come in through Lake Pontchartrain, and New Orleans would be on the east side of the eye—the side that contained more rain. A normal downpour always flooded the streets on the east side, so the pumping system would already be working hard to pump the water out when the storm-surge came into the lake and rushed into the canals looking for a way out. All we could do was pray the levees held this time.

At five-fifty, Paige chased Nicky down and placed him, struggling and howling, into his cat carrier.

"I'm going to put him in the car and then do one last check around here," she said.

I listened to the news one last time. The eye was now projected to come ashore near Grand Isle, where a solitary man refused to evacuate. Grand Isle was almost completely destroyed by Katrina, and already the sea level was starting to rise. This was very bad news for Lafourche and Terrebonne parishes, which took a beating not only during Katrina but also during Hurricane Rita a few weeks later. The Louisiana Gulf Coast had not fully recovered from that one-two punch during the horrible hurricane season of 2005, which remained the worst on record.

I hit the OFF button, and the television screen went black. I heard footsteps coming up the stairs. The door opened.

"You'd never know there was a storm coming," Paige said. "It's hot out there, but such a beautiful day."

"It was beautiful the last time," I said.

Paige walked around the house, checking windows to make sure they were closed. She went through the refrigerator again, and carried the bag of perishables to be discarded to the front door.

"Seems kind of silly to put this in the garbage," she said. "It'll just blow away. But I don't want this shit to rot in the house. I'll check upstairs and then we can go, okay?"

I reflected on our situation while she moved around upstairs. Ginevra wouldn't come ashore until around six the next day. We had twenty-four hours to get to Houston. A full tank should get us both there, even at the gas-guzzling crawl we were expecting.

Paige gave me a shaky smile as she came downstairs.

"This is it."

I took her in my arms and we held each other for a few moments, and then she broke away from me. I went out the door first. She slammed it shut with a loud clang that startled me in the silence. I put my key in the car door and turned it, pulling on the handle.

That's odd, I thought. *I was sure I locked it when I got here.*

But I couldn't swear to it. It was something I did reflexively, and I'd had a lot on my mind when I'd pulled up.

I looked in the backseat. Nothing seemed to be missing.

I put the key in the ignition and gave it a little gas.

Nothing.

All the dummy lights came on. I slammed my fist on the steering wheel, turning the key again.

Nothing. Not even that annoying *rrrrr-rrrrr-rrrrr* that signified a dying battery.

But if the battery was dead, the dummy lights wouldn't come on.

I popped the hood, got out, and slammed the car door shut just as Paige opened her car door and called back to me, "Stupid son of a bitch won't start."

My body went cold, despite the humidity.

"Pop your hood," I called as I lifted mine.

My distributor cap was gone, and so was Paige's.

Vinnie hadn't left town. We were trapped in an empty city with a hurricane on its way—and a professional killer about to pounce.

CHAPTER FOURTEEN

I DID A QUICK 360-degree turn, scanning the immediate area as I shouted at Paige to get down. I dropped to
my knees, scrutinizing the big brick apartment building across the street. If he was in there, we were easy
targets.

But he wouldn't be behind one of those windows,
peering through the blinds. A professional would first
make sure he had a clear shot. His second priority
would be to ensure easy access to the target, in case he
missed that first shot. The third priority was a clear and
easy escape route. I could rule out the massive apartment building. If he missed a shot from there, we'd be
able to escape while he came down to the street. If Vinnie was still here—and undoubtedly he was—he had to
be on the same side of the street as Paige's house. He
would have to come get us.

I reached up and opened my car door, keeping my
head down, and retrieved the gun in the armrest between the front seats. As I shut my car door I glanced

over at Paige, who was getting hers. Sweat rolled into my eyes.

I dialed Venus from stored numbers on my cell phone, and swore under my breath when I got the circuits-busy message yet again. Fingers shaking, I sent a text—*SOS P & I stranded cars dead Vinnie here SOS*—and said a brief prayer that Venus and Blaine would come soon.

I scuttled along the side of my car to the back fender and made a hurried scan of the house next door and the ones beyond. All the windows were empty. I pulled my head back and moved to the front bumper of the car. Paige was at the back fender of hers.

"Nothing at the house next door," she said, her voice low. "Where do you think he is?"

I ran over the geography of Paige's house again in my mind. The fences were high, with razor wire on top. Even with a ladder, the drop down would be at least seven feet. He'd have to jump across and come down on the concrete, and risk breaking a leg or spraining an ankle. From Paige's side of the house, we'd hear him. It had to be the house to the left, which had a parking area that led to the back of the house. I couldn't remember if the backyard was fenced off from the lot. Blaine and I had focused on access to Paige's lot. There was also no way of knowing when Vinnie took the distributor caps. He may have come over the fence at any time after I arrived, and we hadn't heard him over the Weather Channel.

He didn't seem interested in coming after us on the street. It was possible we could make a break for it, run the few blocks to my apartment, barricade ourselves in there, and wait for help. But if we did that, we'd be in the open crossing Coliseum Square. Even if we made it safely across the park, we'd be sitting ducks while I unlocked the door. There was no way of knowing how long it would take for help to arrive. Hopefully, this would be seen as enough of an emergency for Venus and Blaine to let their colleagues attend to looters and evacuating the city.

But we couldn't count on that. Nor could we stay cowering behind our cars. To get out of range, we simply had to make it to the corner and around the building there. We could also try for the Avenue Pub, almost the exact same distance in the other direction. I discarded that option immediately. Vinnie would have no problem killing us and eliminating any customers who might be there, if the pub were even open. It was bad enough Paige was in danger.

The best option was to make a break for Paige's apartment. It was only a few yards to the gate and then to the safe side of the house. Her landline was working; we could try Venus again from inside. Her Internet was also working, and the apartment was practically a fortress. The windows were too high off the ground for someone on foot to reach, and even with a ladder he'd have to break one to get in, which we would hear. By the time he was inside we'd be on him, guns drawn. The only other way in was to kick down the first floor door—again, we'd be ready. Blaine had worried about the second floor patio, but I didn't see how Vinnie could get in that way without us hearing, either.

The problem was that we'd be trapped inside. Still, it was the only way to buy enough time for Blaine and Venus to save us.

"We have to get back inside your apartment, Paige," I said.

"I can't leave Nicky out here, Chanse. It's too hot. He'll die without water."

"We need to go fast, Paige. Lugging the carrier will make us sitting ducks."

"I'll get him out of the carrier."

Before I could object, she crab-walked to the back door of her car. I stuck my head out between the cars to reconnoiter our escape route. If I opened the gate and got to the porch, Paige could run to her door and open it for me. If Vinnie was in the house next door, he had no good angle on us. We could make it. Paige gripped Nicky firmly with both arms while I told her the plan, her gun tucked in the back of her jeans. Nicky hid his head in her armpit.

Clutching the key to the gate in my left hand and my gun in the right, I crawled between the cars, dashed for the gate, shoved the key in the lock, twisted it right, and heard the lock disengage. I shoved the gate open and dashed up the stairs, flattening myself against the door to John and Michael's apartment. The gate clanged shut. I jumped over the side railing and stayed down until I was on the side of the house, then ran back to Paige's apartment, shut the door behind me, and twisted the deadbolt.

I leaned against the door in time to see the white and orange flurry of Nicky scampering up the stairs.

Paige gave me a thumbs-up as she connected with Venus on the telephone and filled her in. She put the phone down and plopped into the reclining chair.

"She's radioing it in," Paige told me. "She doesn't know how long it will take. I'm sorry, Chanse, we should have evacuated as soon as you got here. It was stupid to wait."

"No, it wasn't," I said, feeling really tired. "The U.S. Marshals told me Vinnie had cleared out, and when nothing happened again, I thought they might be right after all. I let down my guard. I'm the one who should be sorry, Paige. When Blaine and I checked out your place the other day, I didn't notice that the backyard next door is easily accessed. Vinnie just needs a ladder to get over the fence. But the only way in here is through the front door, so we should be okay."

"You forgot the patio. My landlady and I share it. The side door to Harriet's apartment is a piece of crap. It's really a set of French doors. They're old and warped, and you have to latch them to make sure they stay closed. The wind can blow them open. If Vinnie gets over the fence, he can come through there."

"Surely she latched them before she evacuated, Paige. She put up razor wire on all the fences to keep out looters. Don't you think she'd have secured the doors against the hurricane?"

"A hard kick would open those doors, Chanse—and I don't know that we'd hear it. They're opposite the front apartment. My patio door isn't secure, either. The knob doesn't latch. I have to use the bolt."

I resisted a brief urge to scream at her. Why hadn't she told us this before? I had a sinking feeling in my stomach.

"What about Harriet's patio door?"

"I don't know."

"Then stay here and guard the stairs while I make sure the upstairs is secure. If Vinnie gets to me, he'll be a perfect target for you."

Paige's face paled, but she nodded. She moved to the couch with her gun.

"I'll shout before I come back down the stairs," I said. "If you hear someone else coming, be ready to shoot."

"Understood. But don't forget to call out—I don't want to cap your ass."

The stairway to the second floor hugged the wall and made a ninety-degree left turn about eight feet up, as you got closer to the ceiling. It made another ninety-degree turn when you passed the ceiling. I started up the stairs, gun ready.

The upstairs hall was empty as I came around the second turn. In the bedroom, Nicky sat on the bed, cleaning himself. He looked at me and made a chirruping sound. The closet door was closed, but I knew it was crammed so full of clothes no one could fit inside. I did a quick sweep of the bathroom. All clear. The patio door was ahead.

Maybe I was overreacting. Vinnie shouldn't know

about the French doors in the apartment next door. He shouldn't know the layout of the house. But he was a professional. I had to assume he'd done his homework.

I slid back the latch. Immediately the door drifted open a few inches. I stepped out onto the patio.

I'd only been on Paige's patio once, when she first moved in and showed me the place. It had been a cloudy day. Being out there in the direct sunlight, I understood why Paige never used it. The patio was bare of furniture and plants—and completely unshaded. It needed a roof and screens to make it usable. Heat radiated upward from the slatted wooden deck. I felt it through my shoes. I looked over the side railing cautiously. It was a long way down. The gallery along the second floor of the carriage house was about four feet lower than the patio, about six feet away. Vinnie was a small man. It was way too far for him to jump up and across.

The other door had to be Harriet's. I turned the knob and the door opened. It was possible that Harriet had forgotten to lock it, but seemed unlikely. My instincts told me Vinnie was inside, waiting.

But what was he waiting for? Harriet's apartment took up an entire side of the house. All Vinnie had needed to do was shoot us from a window in the front room facing the street. Why hadn't he done it?

That was when I smelled the smoke.

I pulled out my cell phone and texted Venus, focusing on keeping my hands steady: *house on fire need help NOW.*

I kicked Harriet's door open and entered the room, both hands on my gun extended before me. The smoke alarm started beeping. Hoping that the alarm was hooked into the fire department, I moved on, into a dimly lit sitting room lined with bookcases. The shutters were closed. I saw smoke coming from the next room, then flames from the burning bed.

Then it dawned on me. The smoke alarms would go off in every apartment in the building. Vinnie had set the fire to drive us outside.

Fuck.

I returned to the patio, holding my shirt over my nose and mouth against the smoke, in time to see a man below scurry around the corner to Paige's side of the house.

Paige screamed.

She must have gone outside when she heard the smoke alarm. I had to stay calm, think clearly. When I reached the side of the house, the overhang of the patio and second floor kept me from getting a shot at Vinnie.

"Where is he?" I heard Vinnie ask sharply.

"He went for help," Paige replied flatly.

"No, he didn't. He's here, inside the house. Come out, MacLeod, or I'll kill her!" he shouted. "You know I'll do it!"

"You're going to kill me anyway," Paige said. "Go ahead and get it over with."

She sounded resigned, submissive.

I was sure it was an act. Paige had faced down men

with guns when she'd worked the crime beat for the *Times-Picayune*. She always kept her head in a crisis. She was distracting Vinnie until I could figure out what to do.

I couldn't go through the burning apartment and come up behind him that way. I couldn't go back into Paige's apartment because that's where he thought I was. I looked at the carriage house gallery.

It was six feet away and four feet down, but the gallery extended all the way to the fences on either side. If I could get across, I'd have a clear shot at Vinnie. But if I jumped, I'd make too much noise, even if I made it. Vinnie would hear me. He'd have a clear shot at me, but he'd have to turn his back on Paige to take it. He'd shoot her first.

The gallery was my only option.

I crept back to Paige's patio door, willing her to keep him talking outside. If he took her inside, one or both of us was dead. I looked around the bathroom but saw nothing that would help. Then I noticed the CD tower in the hallway.

Paige had gotten rid of all her CD's years ago, when she bought her iPod, but she'd kept the tower because it was hand-carved from solid wood. I remembered her telling me about some monastery in one of the coastal parishes where the monks were woodworkers. It was about seven feet high and two feet wide. I picked it up. It was heavy, but I could manage it. Would it support my weight? For that matter, would the railings?

I had no choice. If I fell, I'd make so much noise that

it would distract Vinnie—and maybe Paige could get a shot off.

I carried it onto the patio, to the corner farthest away from Paige's side of the building. My arms and shoulders strained as I hoisted the case and lowered it carefully across the space between the buildings. Sweat poured down my face. My body screamed from the effort to hold it steady. Finally, I set it down gently on the opposite railing. I climbed onto the patio railing, put my knees on the horizontal tower, and began to stand up. The railings trembled. I gritted my teeth. My entire body was shaking. I willed it to stop as I rose to my full height. A gust of wind hit me. I struggled to maintain my balance, trying to grasp the tower with my toes through my shoes.

I wiped the sweat from my hands and took a deep breath to steady myself, then let out the breath and scrambled across as quickly as I could. With every step, the railings shook. The tower trembled a bit, but held.

I could hear their voices as I stepped gratefully onto the carriage house gallery. They were still outside.

"COME OUT MACLEOD! YOURE JUST MAKING IT WORSE FOR YOURSELF!"

I moved cautiously along the gallery, gun ready, until I had a clear view of Vinnie's back. Paige was looking at him. She didn't see me.

I took aim and pulled the trigger three times.

Paige screamed as Vinnie's body jerked from the impact of the bullets. Without another sound, he collapsed on the paving stones. I dropped my gun and sat down hard, trying to catch my breath. I closed my eyes and rested my head on my knees.

Then I heard another shot.

I jumped up and raised my gun, and then relaxed.

Paige was standing over Vinnie. She'd blown off half his head. His blood was splattered all over her. She looked up at me.

"Took you long enough," she said.

Her eyes rolled backward and she fainted.

Paige was already sitting up by the time I reached her.

"Can you stand?" I asked.

She looked at me, dazed, then got to her feet. I put my arm around her.

"Thanks, Chanse," she said softly.

I helped her walk alongside the house. We reached the front just as a fire truck pulled up. I set Paige down on the steps and unlocked the gate.

"It's the other side of the house, upstairs," I called out as the firemen trooped past us.

"The house—Nicky—"

"Get his carrier from the car," I said, "and I'll go and find him."

Nicky gave me a head butt when I grabbed him from the coffee table where he was sitting. On the steps, Paige scooped him into her arms and buried her face in his thick fur. I sat down beside them, exhausted.

"You two have certainly gotten yourselves into a fine fix," Blaine drawled.

"Took you two long enough to get here," I retorted. "Vinnie's body is back there. Go earn your pay."

Blaine radioed for backup and the Crime Lab, and headed around the house. Venus sat down next to me.

"You both okay?"

I nodded.

She patted me on the arm. "I'll be right back."

Two hours later, the body was gone, the crime scene photos taken. Paige and I had typed up statements on her laptop and signed them. The fire hadn't taken long to put out—only the mattress was burning. Paige had showered and changed her clothes.

The sun was setting. Dark clouds massed in the south.

"You two need to get out of town," Blaine said, handing us a couple of keys from his key ring. "Take my Bronco. It's fully gassed and parked at the house. Just be careful with it, okay?"

Blaine and Venus drove me over to Blaine's place on the other side of Coliseum Square from my apartment, and we took our leave of each other.

"Be careful, you two," I said.

"The storm keeps moving west," Venus said as she climbed back into their car. "We're going to get hit, but it may not be as bad as they thought."

"Hallelujah," I said, and waved at them as they drove off.

It took us about an hour, but somehow we fit everything from both cars into the Bronco. We even managed to keep the backseat clear. The last thing to go in was Nicky's carrier. He howled his displeasure as soon as it was secured.

Paige fastened her seat belt as I turned the key in the ignition. Lights on, we headed for St. Charles Avenue and out of the city.

EPILOGUE

As PAIGE AND I spent an aggravating and tense twelve hours on I-10 West to Houston, the hurricane continued turning. At eight p.m. on Sunday, in my sister's living room, Paige and I watched Ginevra come ashore eighty miles west of New Orleans. The storm-surge into the Lake Borgne–Rigolets–Lake Pontchartrain system was lower than originally predicted, but still dangerous.

And the levees held.

We returned home four days later, after power was restored to our neighborhood. New Orleans was slightly damaged—trees down or denuded of branches, some roofs gone, windows broken—but our beautiful city had survived.

Unfortunately, Vernita did not.

She was processed very quickly that Saturday, and released on her own recognizance. (As Venus told us later, "The system didn't want to be responsible for on older lady being jailed during a hurricane.") Apparently

Cordelia was able to pull strings even with a Category 3 bearing down on the city.

But not even Cordelia could prevent the series of strokes Vernita suffered once they reached the Sheehans' home in Baton Rouge. She died early Sunday morning.

I don't know whether Alais was ever told that Jerrell was her half-brother, nor do I care.

I cashed the Sheehans' check. I figured out how much they owed me at my regular rate, and returned the rest to Loren McKeithen's office.

There's talk around town that Janna Sheehan might run for the Senate. I'm not sure how I feel about that, but if the choice is between Janna and that man from Metairie, she's got my vote.

Despite my desire to have nothing more to do with the Sheehan family, one nice thing came out of the case. About a week after Ginevra, Rory Delesdernier called me and asked for a date. I decided to take a chance, and said yes. We'll see how that goes.

I never had the chance to get my hands on Special Agent Palladino, but I'm sure our paths will cross again someday.

I not only gave Abby a raise, I made her a partner. She really is a natural at this kind of work—and better to have her working by my side than competing against me.